DEADLY SINS
COMPLETE
A DEZERAY JACKSON MINI-SERIES

Kori D. Miller

Back Porch Writer Press

FREMONT, NEBRASKA

Back Porch Writer Press
2570 County Road 12
Fremont, NE 68025
www.backporchwriter.com

Publisher's Note: This is a work of fiction. Names, characters, places, and incidents are a product of the author's imagination. Locales and public names are sometimes used for atmospheric purposes. Any resemblance to actual people, living or dead, or to businesses, companies, events, institutions, or locales is completely coincidental.

Book Layout © 2014 BookDesignTemplates.com

Deadly Sins Complete: A Dezeray Jackson Mini-Series/ Kori D. Miller. -- 1st ed.
ISBN 978-0-9914756-3-6

For SLE

People under suspicion are better moving than at rest.

—FRANZ KAFKA

CONTENTS

CHAPTER ONE

GAMERS IN PARADISE

"Damn it!" I scooped up the ketchup, trying not to smear it. Another shirt bites the dust. I looked up just in time. My target stepped out of his apartment. He made a beeline for a late-model blue Ford pickup parked across the street. His backpack sagged on his shoulders.

"Yo, man, hurry up!" A young guy yelled to him from the driver's side of the truck.

"Don't sweat it, man. I'm comin'." He got in.

I followed them as they drove the two blocks to the driver's one-story, orange-sided duplex. The street-side windows were always open. It was the same story every day. I grabbed my camera, took a couple of shots, and then set it aside.

"This shit is getting old," I muttered to no one.

Tracer International, my employer, assigned me to what I concluded was the most uneventful, boring case possible. It was some sort of punishment. Richter, my boss, was still a little pissed. How was I supposed to know his wife was a gold-digging slut intent on embezzling from the company? I didn't hire her. Their divorce was quick.

Our client was an older woman with a loser for a grandson. She'd supported the ingrate for years, and was, according to her file, tired. She wanted to know how he spent his time. Millicent James knew he was lying to her, but couldn't prove it, and for some reason, couldn't cut the apron strings. She believed that if she knew the truth, then she could walk away. Whatever floats your boat, I guess. I would have kicked his lazy ass to the curb long before now.

I thumbed through the file, again. A picture dropped out. The guy in the picture wore an over-sized plaid, button-down shirt and faded jeans. His dark hair was short. There was something about his crooked grin that set me off. I didn't like him. It was a feeling I got. It was kind of like when you get stuck in a grocery line behind a toddler who just shit his pants. The odor reaches your nostrils. Your stomach twists. The bile comes just to the upper part of your throat, and you choke it back.

A few hours passed. The Miami humidity kicked in, so I started the car and clicked on the air. I hated Miami. Five years tracing and tailing dumb-asses were taking their toll. Tracer International paid for my housing, so I stashed away most of my check. I was ready for a change.

"Yo, man, calm down!" My target, Carver Stewart, tripped backward down the short flight of stairs to the sidewalk. "I'll get it for you."

I rolled down my window. A guy I'd never seen before stood in the door. He started toward Stewart. The driver was in step behind him. I picked up my "point and click" and took a few more shots.

"I don't have time for your shit!" He grabbed Stewart.

"Really, man, I can get it."

The man shoved Stewart aside. "You've got two days." The man went inside. The driver shrugged his shoulders at Stewart and followed the other man.

Stewart pulled out his phone. A few minutes later, a red Firebird stopped in front of the duplex. An average-sized brunette sat behind the wheel. Stewart got in. I followed them the two blocks back to Stewart's place.

*****

Millicent James lived in an upper middle-class neighborhood called Pinecrest. Technically, it's a village, but to me, it was just another place. The houses were large, the yards well-tended, and nearly every face was white. There were exceptions, but none of them lived there.

I rolled my car up a long, brick driveway flanked by palm trees, into a large courtyard. I parked my Explorer in front, hoping the oil leak was actually fixed this time. The doorbell banged. I expected a chime for some reason. Millicent James opened the door.

"Ms. Jackson, come in." She led me to a sitting room to the left of the main entrance. Glasses of lemonade waited on a table. "Please, sit down. Make yourself comfortable."

"Mrs. James."

"Oh, call me Millie." She waved me off for being so formal.

She was a nice old lady. "Millie, I have reason to believe your grandson might be in a bit of trouble."

"What kind of trouble?" She sat on a white couch opposite me.

"I'm not sure yet. Do you know any of his friends?"

She thought for a minute. Her right hand covered her mouth. "Hmmm. Only two. He has a girlfriend named Cindy, and I know he brought a young man by once or twice. Let me think. Let me think." She looked away. "Oh yes, Thomas! Yes, that's it."

I placed a few pictures on the table between us. "Is this Thomas?" I pointed to the smaller of two guys. The one that picked up Stewart the other day.

"Yes, I believe it is."

"Do you know who the other man is?"

"No, I'm afraid I don't."

I placed another picture onto the table. "Is this Cindy?"

"Yes. She's a lovely girl."

The front door slammed shut. We both stood. Carver Stewart walked past the sitting-room doorway.

"Carver?" Mrs. James said.

He returned, but didn't enter the room.

"Where have you been? I called you several times, dear."

Stewart looked me over. There was a hint of recognition, but he couldn't place who I was.

"Nowhere, Grams. I was hangin' with Thomas, that's all. I'm gonna get something to eat." He disappeared down the hall.

*****

The body of Millicent James, of Pinecrest, was found in her bedroom early this morning by her housekeeper. Sources close to the investigation say that Mrs. James died of an apparent overdose. The Pinecrest Village police declined to offer any specific details about the crime, and indicated that their investigation is underway.

I set down my can of Coke and turned up the volume on my TV.

Mrs. James is the widow of famed entrepreneur and inventor Simon James. It's rumored that her estate is worth $10 million. Her family could not be reached for comment. Stay tuned to this station for updates.

I turned off the TV, grabbed my keys, and headed to Pinecrest. It took 45 minutes in morning traffic to get from my place in Kendall to her place. I hate Miami.

As expected, I couldn't get too close; the police had the road closed in both directions for half a block. But I wanted to see who showed up. In my experience, the perp usually likes to watch things unfold. It's a little like "who smelt it, dealt it." I was looking for that person. The over-the-top doer of the deed. I saw a red Firebird. I parked a few cars away from it. Cindy waited inside. Now, I knew where Stewart was. The only question was, did he ever leave?

After about an hour, Cindy received a phone call. A few minutes later, Carver Stewart waved to her from the James' driveway. She started the car and pulled around to pick him up. A police officer moved the barricade. I waited a few beats, then followed them out of Pinecrest.

They drove straight to Stewart's neighborhood, but stopped at Thomas' place. There were plenty of cars parked along the street, so I pulled in behind one, cut the engine, and rolled down the window to wait. Stewart stepped out of the car and headed to the door. The big guy beat him to it.

"I got it. I got it." Stewart put his hands up.

The big guy grabbed Stewart and pushed him inside.

An hour passed before Stewart reappeared. He slung his backpack over his shoulder. No more sag. He whistled to Cindy. She started the engine, turned the car around, and met him at the curb.

I thought they'd head to his place, but they didn't. I followed them to Tropical Park. They located a parking spot. Stewart got out of the car. I grabbed my camera, locked the car, and strolled along behind him. I pretended to take nature pictures as we walked the paths. He led me to a hidden lake with very few people. I kept walking, but backtracked and hid behind trees.

Stewart opened his backpack. I used my camera to zoom in for a better view. A medicine bottle. What a shit! I started taking pictures. I couldn't stop him, but at least I could show what he had in his hands, and when he had it.

He filled the small bottle with rocks. Replaced the cap, and tossed it into the lake. On the way back to the Firebird, he made a call. He laughed. Asshole.

*****

I wasn't sure what I wanted to do with my pictures of Stewart at the lake. I should hand everything over to the police. That was the prudent thing to do. It was their investigation. That's what I was supposed to do. Richter would be even angrier if I skirted company protocol. That thought caused a smile to creep across my face.

The drive to Stewart's neighborhood took 20 minutes from where I was in Kendall. It was late, so traffic was light. I had no real plan for when I got there. I still didn't know what that big guy wanted, and now had, thanks to Stewart. I did know it had something to do with Millie. After a month of watching Stewart, I didn't see him working too hard to do anything, except sit on his ass playing games. Whatever he did, it had to be simple, and he had to be getting something pretty great from it.

As I drove down his street, I saw that his place was completely dark. I parked, grabbed a penlight I kept in the glove box, and stepped out. His apartment was on the main floor. There was one bay window in the front, two smaller windows along the south side of the fourplex, and a small kitchen window in the back. The only door to his place was at the front, near the entrance to the building. There was an exit at the back of the hallway that lead to a small, tenant-parking area. Both main doors were locked.

There was no activity in the front. I walked along the south side. One thing about young guys — they're not into curtains. The blinds were open. Soda cans, pizza boxes, and chip bags littered the living room. An entertainment cabinet spanned the length of one wall. There were two wide-screen TVs, four or five game stations, and various controllers. I continued to the next window — his bedroom. A futon bed rested on the wood floor. Clothes were scattered around the room. And along one wall there was another entertainment center, with one wide-screen TV, two game stations and various controllers. I hope he gets paid for doing this crap.

I returned to my truck. There were only two places Stewart would be at this hour. I drove two blocks to Thomas' place. Lights from a TV flickered in the front room. After I parked, I crept around to the side of the duplex. There were several windows. Looking through the first one, I saw Stewart, Thomas, and the big guy lounging on beanbags in front of four wide-screen, wall-mounted TVs. What the hell is wrong with these people?

The window was open to catch a nonexistent breeze.

"See, what'd I tell you?" Stewart reached for a beer on the floor next to him. "Limited edition, prerelease." He raised his beer to the screen.

"Yeah, this is the game," Thomas answered.

"It's the shit, that's for sure," the big guy said.

"She didn't know what she had — couldn't appreciate the gift." Stewart took a long pull from the bottle.

"That's just cold, man." The big guy adjusted his beanbag. "If it was my grams, I'd be upset."

"I can't get too bent outa shape. She was old. Besides, I'm sure she's in a better place."

I'd heard enough. After I got into my car, I googled "Simon James." There it was in Wikipedia.

Simon James, entrepreneur and inventor, owner of Simon Electronics & Games.

I knew that part, but further down, I learned that the company created the game Stewart and his buddies were playing. It was Mission: Kill On Sight, scheduled for release in two months.

Millie sold the company after her husband died. She hated gaming. Most of her money was actually the result of the sale. She'd told us that during our initial consultation a month ago. Go, Millie. The company must have sent her a prerelease.

*****

The dots were all lining up. It was time to go to the police. But first, I had to tell Richter.

"What the hell were you thinking?" Richter stood. His chair rolled back, hitting the credenza behind it.

"Look, I knew something wasn't right, and I followed my instincts."

"Well, you can follow your instincts out the fucking door! Jeopardizing our reputation with local authorities? You know better." He ran his hand through his thinning hair. I couldn't help but think, *You shouldn't do that. There's not much left.* I stifled a grin. "What? This is amusing to you? That's it. After you file your report, pack your shit, and get out. You're done."

"Richter, come on. Seriously? This is about your wife, isn't it?"

He walked around his desk. I gave him a little space.

"This isn't about her."

"How about a transfer? You're happy. I'm happy. All's good."

He leaned back and sat on the edge of his desk. "Fine. A transfer without a recommendation."

"I can live with that."

I left his office. You know how after a long ordeal people say, "It was like a giant weight was lifted?" They're right. I damn near skipped to my desk.

My report filed, and Stewart in custody a few days later, I was ready to pack my apartment. New York City was a short flight, but I opted to drive. Everything I owned fit into the back of my Explorer.

The local news went crazy over the story. Stewart confessed. The day I saw him at her place, he stayed over. Millie kept the game in a safe in her bedroom. He went into her room while she was sleeping, but she woke up. He told her he heard something and came to check on her. When she asked him to hand her the prescription sleeping pills she kept in her bathroom, he handed her three. She was groggy, and didn't notice. The extra dosage interfered with her other medications and caused heart failure. The pill bottle he tossed into the lake was for the sleeping pills. The coroner's report indicated she'd taken them, but the police couldn't find the bottle, until I provided the pictures. In every interview he said, "I didn't mean to kill her. I only wanted her to sleep through the night." Well, he won't be sleeping through too many nights where he's going.

What a complete dumbass. Millie came to us after she updated her will designating him as the primary beneficiary. Apparently, she didn't share that detail with Stewart. He had everything. All she asked him to do was get a job.

CHAPTER TWO

WHIP IT

I opted to walk the four blocks from my apartment to the New York City office of Tracer International. It was my last day. By this time tomorrow, I'd be heading to Omaha, NE. A free house was an offer I couldn't refuse. And, Omaha would be a welcome change of pace.

"Dez." Sam Walters greeted me as I stepped out of the elevator on the 20th floor.

"Sam." I kept walking. He tagged along. The office was like every other place I'd worked. The elevator door opened and the reception desk was all you saw. To the right, a door led to the back offices and cubicles for entry-and mid-level investigators. That was me. I waved my ID in front of the sensor. There was a click, and the lock released.

"You've got one more assignment. Becker dropped it on your desk an hour ago."

I checked my watch. It was 7:30 a.m.

"He said I should go along with you."

I stopped at my desk. A file rested in the center. I'd cleaned everything else out last night, not that it amounted to much after two years. It all fit in a shoebox. I opened the file.

"It's a stolen-property case. The client doesn't want the police involved. I'm not sure why." Sam plopped down in a chair next to my desk. He was an entry-level investigator.

"Sasha Alexander? Why do I know that name?" I asked more to myself than to Sam, but he spoke up anyway.

"Socialite. She owns a gallery in SOHO." He twirled a pencil between his fingers.

"Wait a minute! Not that gallery?"

"One and the same." He grinned.

"Christ." I dropped the file. "Let's go."

We grabbed a taxi. Screw the trains. It was my last day. Company-paid expenses are a privilege I'd be without in about 24 hours.

Alexander's gallery fit in perfectly with all the others in SOHO until you walked through the doors. I paused on the street in front and took a deep breath.

"Let's go!" Sam, always the eager one, reached for the handle. People pushed past me on the sidewalk. I followed Sam through large, ornately-carved wood doors into a small alcove. Heavy, plush, red drapes hung from the ceiling, blocking our view.

Sam pulled one of the drapes aside, allowing me to enter the gallery.

"Oy," I mumbled, and took it all in at once. Some things can't be unseen.

"Wow" was all Sam could manage to say.

*****

"Oh, hello. I'm Tish." A tall, twig-like blonde woman greeted us as she walked past a phallic sculpture in the center of the gallery. The sculpture was surrounded by hands at its base, and several half-way up its length appeared to squeeze it, making a milky liquid ooze from its top. "Isn't it magnificent?" She paused to admire the sculpture. "It's our newest addition to the gallery."

She held out her hand. I wasn't sure I wanted to shake it.

"My name is Dezeray Jackson. This is my associate, Sam Walters. We're here to speak with Sasha Alexander."

"And, you're with?" She tilted her head. It reminded me of a dog trying to figure something out.

"Tracer International."

"I see. Follow me, please."

We walked around the giant penis and down a short hallway, passing two doors before reaching what I assumed was Alexander's office.

Tish popped her head into the office, careful not to open the door completely. "Sasha, they're here." She closed the door. "She'll be right with you." Tish disappeared down the hallway.

A minute later, a brunette opened the door. She was about 5'7".

"Please, come in."

Her office was more like a Moroccan-style boudoir. Silk burgundy-colored drapes created a billowing effect over the ceiling. There were large, overstuffed pillows on the floor, and long, backless couches arranged in a sitting area. Etched metal lanterns cast shadows and designs around the room. A shirtless man lounged on a couch, his well-tanned muscles covered in an oily sheen.

"I apologize if we've interrupted something," I said.

"Not at all." She walked to the man and sat near his head. She picked up a small whip from the table in front of her. It wasn't more than six inches long. There were beads tied to the end of each small, leather strip. "Please, sit."

Sam moved to a couch opposite the couple. Droplets of sweat formed on his upper lip. I remained standing. Alexander smacked the whip on the man's chest, and moved it up and down from his chest to his navel. She repeated the action, increasing the intensity of the slap each time. The man smiled. She stared at Sam.

"Hhem. I understand that something was stolen from your collection last night," I said.

Without looking at me, she said. "Yes. Something from my private collection." The whip slapped harder. The man groaned. Sam shifted in his seat.

"You didn't specify what was stolen."

She smacked the man, again. He groaned louder. His silk pants began to shift near his crotch. It was time to wrap this up.

"It was a leather whip."

"A whip?"

She looked at me. "Yes. A gold-handled, leather whip with diamonds sewn into the strands all the way to the end. It's approximately 6 feet long." Smack! "It's valued at $200,000." She leaned forward, picked up a file from the table, and handed it to Sam. She leaned back, crossed her legs, and said, "There's a picture in the file."

"Any idea who'd want to take your, uh, whip?" I asked.

"I don't share my personal collection with many people. Only a select few would truly appreciate it." Her gaze returned to Sam. He stood up and headed for the door. "I took the liberty of including a brief list of names for you to investigate. You only have 24 hours to find it."

"What happens after 24 hours?"

"The game is over."

Outside, Sam handed me the file. There were three names: Sophia Charles, Michael Bowers, and Miles Vincent. Each person had a few things in common. They were all young, wealthy, apparently into S and M, and playing some sort of game. Yay, me. Alexander provided their photos and contact information.

"Let's start with Miles Vincent. He lives near here. The other two are in the Village."

"Dez, he's probably at work."

I looked at Sam, eyebrow raised, and said, "Really? You think he's working?"

Vincent's place was a few blocks from Alexander's gallery. I was getting a lot of exercise my last day in the city. The doorman rang Vincent's apartment. After a few minutes he directed us to a private elevator. His apartment was at the top, of course. One thing about young, wealthy socialite types — they're predictable.

"You must be the folks from Tracer International." A tall, lean man approached us, extending his hand. His grip was strong.

"Yes. I'm Dez ..."

"Dezeray Jackson." He smiled, revealing perfectly-spaced, very white teeth.

"And," he turned toward Sam, "Sam Walters. Please, come in. Can I get you anything to drink?"

We followed him into a spacious, sunken living room. Plush, white couches and pillows were arranged in a semicircle with a rectangular glass table within arm's reach of every seat. As we moved closer, I realized that the base of the table was of two intertwined bodies.

"No, thank you. We're fine," I answered. Sam stared at the table.

"I know Sasha is desperately searching for her prized possession." He retrieved a glass of white wine from a nearby bar, and rejoined us in the living room.

"Please, make yourselves comfortable." He motioned to one of the couches.

"What do you know about the whip?" I asked.

"Well, I know I'm not crazy enough to steal it in the middle of a game." He sipped his wine. "Those are lovely shoes."

I looked down. I forgot I was wearing sandals, and for once, I'd opted to polish my toenails.

"Red. It suits you." He was talking about the polish, not the shoes. What the hell? What kind of man notices toenail polish? The moment I thought it, I knew the answer. Shit.

"Mr. Vincent, if you didn't steal it, who do you think did? And, what's this game you're playing, anyway?"

His fingers danced around the rim of his wine glass. "Tsk. Tsk. If you're not a member, I'm afraid that I can't tell you." He leaned forward. His dark eyes hooded by their lids. "Would you like to become a member?"

*****

We needed to eat. We stopped at a pizza joint to grab a slice, and walked a bit.

"What the fuck is wrong with these people?"

This was the most I'd heard from Sam since we left the gallery.

"Oh, I don't know. I thought you kinda liked Sasha. She's certainly fond of you." I stifled a laugh.

"Jesus Christ, these people are into some strange shit."

"Maybe, but that's not our problem. Stay focused, Sam." I tossed my napkins into a can near the corner and hailed a taxi. We headed to The Village to track down Sophia Charles and Michael Bowers.

Charles' place was a chic walk-up between a tattoo parlor and a jazz joint. No bellman. No private elevator. Maybe this one was different. She answered the door wearing nothing but a knee-length, sheer nightgown. Maybe not.

I glanced at Sam. "You know what, Sam. I think it would be best if you waited outside for this one." He diverted his eyes, shook his head, and headed for the stairs.

"I'll be at the coffee place on the corner."

"May I help you?" Ms. Charles opened the door to allow me a better view.

"My name is Dezeray Jackson. I'm with Tracer International. I believe you're familiar with our client, Sasha Alexander."

"Well, of course I am. Please, come in."

It was nearly one o'clock in the afternoon. "I realize it's early, and you obviously haven't had a chance to get dressed. I can wait a few minutes while you do that." I smiled.

"Oh, don't be silly. I'm fine." She walked down a short hall. "Make yourself comfortable. I'll just get us something to drink."

Pictures of naked bodies covered every wall in her living room. One caught my attention. In it, a woman rested on her elbows with her back arched and head back. It looked as though water rushed over her body and left bits of sparkling sand in its wake. A man crouched between her legs. The woman was Ms. Charles. I scanned all the pictures. They were all of her in various sexual positions or trysts.

"That was a wonderful afternoon." She returned from the kitchen with two glasses of red wine.

"Uh, huh." I walked toward a window overlooking the street. "Ms. Charles, you're probably already aware that someone stole an artifact from Ms. Alexander's collection."

"Yes, but I don't know how I could possibly help you. We're in the middle of a game. Why would I take it?" She motioned to the various pictures. "As you can see, I prefer pleasure."

"Yeah, okay. Where were you last night?"

She stepped closer to me, and brushed my curls back, revealing my neck. "I was right here. All night." She sipped her wine. I moved away.

"Were you alone?"

"As a matter of fact, I wasn't. Michael joined me last night."

"Michael Bowers?"

"The very one." She pointed at a picture on a table next to the couch. "That's him. As you can see, he's worth losing a little sleep over."

In the picture, Bowers posed naked with a rose between his teeth, and a small, black-leather whip in his hands.

"It seems that Mr. Bowers appreciates pleasure and pain."

"Yes, he does." She moved closer to me. "What about you Ms. Jackson? Do you prefer pleasure or pain?" Her hand reached up to stroke my face. I stopped it.

"You're not my type, Ms. Charles."

I found Sam at the coffee shop, grabbed a coke, and headed for Bowers' place. It was a few blocks from Ms. Charles' apartment. And, his place had a doorman. On the way, I let Sam in on the details of my chat, leaving out the "she came onto me part," but including the picture of Bowers with the whip.

"What I don't get is this $200K whip, and how it's connected to whatever game they're playing," Sam said. We rode the elevator to the top floor.

"Me, either."

The elevator door opened, revealing a dimly-lit entryway. Sconces created flickering shadows. A large bear-skin rug lay in the middle of the room. Animal heads were mounted along the walls at various heights. Giant antlers hung above the front door. Here we go.

"Okay, so maybe he's a hunter," Sam said, as the door opened.

"No, I simply appreciate these magnificent creatures. Enter."

"Mr. Bowers, my name is ..."

"I know who you are."

He led us into a candle-lit living room. Large, ornately-carved chairs, a brown leather sofa, and more animal pelts adorned the space. At the far end of the room was a wood-burning fireplace. I could have stood in it. Heavy, brown drapes covered the windows from the ceiling to the floor. More sconces flickered. Baroque music played in the background. Despite the burning fire, the room was cold.

"Sit." He motioned to the couch.

Sam sat.

"I'll stand, thanks."

A smile played on his lips. His right brow rose. "I see."

"Mr. Bowers, I'm just going to come out and ask. Do you have Ms. Alexander's whip?"

"No, I don't, but if I did, I'd love to make use of it with you."

Sam stood. I looked at him and shook my head. "Sam." He sat back down.

"Yeah, that's not really my thing."

He walked closer. "Really? I bet it is."

I stepped back. Sam stood between us. "Sir, you need to move away from Ms. Jackson."

"It's okay, Sam."

"Yes, Sam, it's okay." His eyes never left mine. "While I enjoy the extraordinary implements of many of our ancestors, I haven't had the pleasure of using Sasha's whip, yet." He smiled.

Then I noticed more of the room. Whips hung on the walls. All different lengths and styles. Some had beads sewn into them, much like what Ms. Alexander had described.

"Tell me about the game."

"There are 10 players."

"What's the objective?"

"To find and bring into the membership, one submissive, in 24 hours."

"And the prize?"

"One million dollars, and one night with Sasha's whip."

"And if Ms. Alexander doesn't have the whip?"

"She becomes a submissive for my pleasure, and the pleasure of all the other dominants. And I for one, am quite — demanding."

We left Bowers' place. It was four o'clock. Something was nagging at my insides, and it wasn't the lingering effect of Bowers' scent — as intoxicating as it was.

"God, I feel like I need a shower," Sam said.

"Different strokes, Sam." I stopped walking. "Let's assess. What do we know?"

"We know these people are freaks, and not just in the bedroom."

I sighed. "We know why someone would take the whip. We also know why Alexander wants it back so badly. And, we know one of these three," I pointed to their pictures in the file, "took it."

We continued walking in silence.

"I got it!"

"What?"

"I know who took it."

We walked back to Ms. Charles' apartment. She opened the door. This time she was dressed in a modest, pale-yellow blouse coordinated with a pencil skirt.

"Oh, Ms. Jackson, I was just about to leave."

"May we come in? It'll only take a minute."

She hesitated. "Yes, but I really only have a moment."

We followed her into the living room. Sam took it all in. "Wow."

She beamed. "They are lovely, aren't they?"

"Where is it?" I asked.

"What are you talking about?"

"The whip. I know you have it, and I know why."

"I don't have the whip."

"Then, you've already given it to your dominant."

I could feel Sam staring at me.

"I don't know what you're talking about." She started for the door. "And, I need to be going." She opened the door to let us out.

"Did he tell you that you'd become a dominant if Sasha became his submissive?"

She closed the door.

"You are Bowers' submissive, right? I'm guessing it happened during a different game. Am I right?"

Ms. Charles walked back into the living room. "Yes, I'm Mr. Bowers' submissive."

"So, he used you to get the whip."

"Yes."

She walked into the kitchen, and returned with a rectangular, wood box. She set it on the dining table, and opened it. The whip was stunning. The gold handle gleamed and the light bounced off the diamonds, creating a massive twinkling effect.

We took the box and left. By eight o'clock we'd delivered it to Sasha Alexander. And, by ten o'clock, I sat in the Paris Cafe bar, in the South Street Seaport neighborhood, for the last time. Sam joined me.

"So, what's next, Dez? I mean, Nebraska? What the hell is in Nebraska?"

"They have a great zoo." I sipped my Guinness. "And, the house is free."

CHAPTER THREE

CODE SWITCH

The dojang smelled. It was an odd combination of sweat, aromatic shoes and dirty socks. It'd been years since I last entered a dojang, and even longer since I'd actually trained with anyone.

Parents sat in folding chairs along the edge of the mats. Some watched and smiled as their children held guns to the chests of other children. Other parents cringed, and busied themselves with their phones, or some other distraction. I suppose watching your 8-year-old hold a gun to another child's head is a bit unsettling, even if it's a rubber gun.

The class ended with a rush of kids and teens making their way to the front to retrieve shoes and school bags. The S.A.F.E. class would begin soon. From what I understood, it was a women's self-defense class. I was skeptical, but came anyway. What could they possibly teach in two hours that a woman would retain and use if attacked? It took years of dedicated training to even hope you'd react the right way. I knew.

I watched the women walk onto the mat. Most came with a buddy. At least they understood one thing: There's safety in numbers. A short, stumpy older man stood in the middle of the room. His students formed a circle around him and he invited the newbies to join. I stayed back. He caught my eye and smiled.

"You're right on time. Good." He greeted me with a handshake and brought me into the circle.

"Everyone, this is Dezeray Jackson. She's a private detective and she knows a thing or two about being attacked. Ms. Walker," he gestured to one of his black belts, "suggested she speak with you tonight."

"Thank you, Mr. Walls. We've all heard the stats. Turn on the TV and you're inundated with story after story about attacks, shootings, domestic violence — the list goes on. The most important thing I can tell you about self-defense is what Mr. Miyagi said: The best defense is not to be there. Don't put yourself in bad situations. Listen to your gut."

"Ms. Jackson, tell the ladies some of your experiences," Mr. Walls said.

"Well, I don't want to take up too much of your time. I'll give you the short version. In my line of work, things can get physical. What I never expected happened years before I became a detective. When I was in college, I met a guy who was all "champagne and roses" in the beginning. By the second month, he became verbally abusive. By the third month, the abuse became physical. It culminated in a knock-em down, drag-em out fight. He finally had me pinned in a corner of my kitchen."

"Ms. Jackson?" A young women, maybe 19 years old, interrupted. "I thought you knew martial arts."

"I did, but I wasn't training regularly at the time. I had the knowledge, but not the speed. Let me be perfectly clear. I was a cocky 20-something martial artist, but I wasn't much of a fighter."

I made eye contact with each newbie. "Just because you're attending this training doesn't mean you'll suddenly know, and be able to use everything right away. You have to be willing to practice. What you learn needs to become embedded in your muscles."

I turned and asked one of the male black belts to attack me from behind, but not to let me know when he'd do it. I faced the young woman again.

"When he pinned me in the corner, all I remember seeing was his knee raising up to my face."

"What did you do?" asked an older woman. I'd put her at about 42 years old. She had remnants of bruising along her left forearm that she kept touching as I spoke.

"I don't remember exactly what I did, but his knee never made contact with my face. The fight ended. I never saw him again, but he was around. He made that known."

*****

"Dez, thanks for doing this on such short notice." Abby Walker was a former high-school friend. We ran into each other at the Y a few months back. She was teaching a kids' karate class. I had watched her demonstrate a series of punches. She looked the same: short brown hair, a smile that lit up a room, and fast as lightning. Back in the day, she was my only competition on the track.

I grabbed my leather backpack. "No problem. I hope it was useful." We walked out. Leaves skirted the sidewalk in swirls until a chilly gust lifted them into the air.

"Damn." I pulled the collar of my coat up and zipped my jacket.

"Wasn't New York City chilly enough for you?"

"In more ways than one. I'm just not ready for winter."

"So, what's next for you?"

Women and students left the karate school in waves. I noticed Ms. Gordan. She hovered near the entrance.

"Not sure. I'm changing my license, but for now, just sort of re-acclimating."

Ms. Gordan scanned the street, then opened the door. She looked at us, said nothing, and began walking north.

"Ms. Gordan?" I followed her with Abby in step behind me.

Ms. Gordan slowed her pace. We caught up to her.

"I'm fine, Ms. Jackson. Really." She turned and walked away. We watched her disappear around the corner at the end of the block.

"Well, that was odd," Abby said.

"Yeah. A bit."

We walked back to our cars. We'd just said our good-byes when the sound of screeching tires pierced the air. The sound came from the block just west of the school. The smell of burnt rubber wafted in the air. Then there was a sort of "thud", and tires screeching, again.

We ran to the end of the block and around the corner. A late model Ford SUV sped away. It was too dark to make out the color.

Ms. Gordan's body lay in the street. Abby fumbled for her phone. I knelt next to Ms. Gordan. Her breathing shallow, she struggled to say something as she reached for my jacket. I leaned closer.

"He's back."

I looked into her blue eyes. "Who's back?"

Her body shuddered. A thin stream of blood trickled from the corner of her mouth. Her hand fell to her side.

Sirens blared in the distance.

"Dez? Dez? Is she?" Abby's voice trembled.

I sat back on my feet. A piece of paper rested on the ground next to my knees.

"She's dead." I stood. The ambulance arrived, followed by the police. I put the paper and my hands into my jacket pockets.

*****

After the police finished their questions, I said goodnight to Abby. I needed a drink. And this time, wine wasn't going to be enough. I got into my low-budget rental car, and headed for O'Malley's Pub. It was a hole in the wall, and usually packed with kids from Creighton University, but on a Tuesday night, it'd be relatively empty, except for a few local old-timers.

I found a seat at the far end of the bar. My backpack rested on the empty chair next to me -- to keep it that way. The gun on my hip nudged my side. I unzipped my jacket and adjusted it.

"What can I get ya?" The bartender's Irish accent had lost its thickness. Too much time in the Midwest, I guessed.

"Redbreast, neat. Thanks."

"Ah, good choice." He retrieved the bottle from behind etched-glass doors and placed a glass in front of me. "You look like you could use a little extra."

I nodded, picked up my glass, and inhaled. Chocolate, laced with a hint of vanilla and spice, soothed my frazzled nerves. One sip. That's all I needed.

A few students stumbled into the bar, followed by a stocky, pale man. The brim of his cap formed a shadow over his eyes. The well-worn leather of his jacket fell heavy on the back of the chair to my left. It smacked my backpack.

"Don't mind if I set this here, do ya?" he asked. His voice was gravelly from what was probably a lifetime of smoking.

Yeah, I did, but as long as he kept his distance, I would let it go.

I shrugged. "Knock yourself out."

He ordered a shot of whiskey — the cheapest they had — and a beer. He knocked the shot back.

"Pretty cold out there ta night, ain't it?" He looked straight ahead.

I decided to ignore him. Maybe he wasn't trying to talk to me. Maybe he was one those guys that liked talking out loud to no one in particular.

"Yeah, winter's gonna be a real bitch. Don't ya think?" he asked.

Okay, so he was trying to talk to me. My "fuck off" sign wasn't bright enough. Damn it.

"I suppose." I took another sip.

"Name's Mike." He turned his stool toward me.

"Uh, huh." My number one rule in situations like this is don't make eye contact. All that does is encourage bad behavior.

"I didn't catch your name."

Seriously? That's his line of choice? I sighed.

"That's because I didn't offer it. Look," I said, still keeping my gaze straight ahead of me, "I don't mean to be rude, but I'm not much for talking right now."

He sat there for a beat, taking in my answer. "What's your deal? I'm just striking up a conversation, that's all. You haven't changed much."

A chill went up my spine. I set my glass down, rolled my shoulders back, and cocked my head to the left and right. I looked at him through the bar mirror. He'd taken off his hat. His straggly hair was still blonde. A smirk twisted the left corner of his mouth. I reached for my bag. He grabbed my hand.

"It's been a long time, Dez."

"You're going to want to let that go."

"Or, what?" He laughed.

I reached for his hand, twisted his wrist and locked it. His chest fell into the bar. The bartender rushed over.

"What's going on here? Is this bum bothering you?"

"I don't know." I looked at Mike. "Are you bothering me?" I grabbed my bag, let go of his hand, and stood. Mike sat up. All eyes were on us. "No, I guess you're not bothering me. Let's keep it that way." I left the bar and headed home. I knew he wouldn't be dumb enough to follow me.

*****

Godfrey greeted me at the door.

"I know, I know, I'm late and you're starving." His big frame circled me. He bumped into my leg. I wobbled, and grabbed the edge of the bookcase near the door. Godfrey raced from the front door to the kitchen. It was a straight shot. He looked back.

"Be patient. Geez. Can I at least get my shoes off?"

He cocked his squarish head to the side. I kicked off my shoes and followed my Rottie's tracks. His bowl filled, Godfrey was a happy dog. I retreated to my bedroom and changed clothes. When I returned to the kitchen, Godfrey was staring at the back door. I let him out. He was a great dog. I lucked out. You never know what you're getting when you rescue a dog.

The grandfather clock, a leftover from my aunt, chimed. It was 9:30 p.m. I grabbed a glass of wine and decided to watch T.V. I must have dozed off because Godfrey's barking woke me with a start. Crap! I left him outside. I peeled myself from the couch. It's a fabulous couch. You sink into it. I checked the clock -- 1:00 a.m. Wow! I went to the kitchen to let him in.

"Come on, Godfrey."

He didn't come.

"Godfrey!"

I heard a low growl.

"Godfrey?"

I shut the door and grabbed the bat I kept propped behind it. This wasn't the best neighborhood. Yeah, I could grab my gun, but that doesn't usually end well, in my experience. Bat in hand, I opened the door, then the screened door. I held it open with my body.

Godfrey." I watched and waited. There wasn't anyone near the fence. At least, not where I could see, but I still couldn't see Godfrey. I reached into the kitchen and clicked off the porch and yard lights. My eyes adjusted. Still nothing.

"Godfrey." I heard a "whoosh" and saw Godfrey chase something across the yard in front of the deck. Whatever it was, got away. Godfrey returned to me, somewhat dejected.

"Next time, Godfrey. Rabbits are fast."

I locked the door behind us and turned the yard lights back on. I was ready for bed.

*****

I rolled over and smacked the alarm. That didn't shut it up. I shoved it off the side table. Crap! I'll be buying another one of those. Godfrey lay in his usual spot, protecting the end of my bed. The damn dog thought he was human.

"Get up, Godfrey. Time to go outside." His eyes barely opened. I walked to the bathroom. Just because he didn't have to go, didn't mean I didn't. When I returned to my bedroom, Godfrey was gone. I walked to the kitchen. Godfrey sat by the door. He looked at me, then at the door.

"You need to learn to open this yourself."

Something on the lawn caught my eye. I put on a pair of boots I kept by the door, and walked down the short flight of steps to the yard. What the hell? Godfrey came over and sat next to me. It looked like a balled up T-shirt with brown spots all over it. I nudged it with the tip of my boot. It fell open. What the fuck?

"Leave it! Stay!" I turned and ran inside.

The police arrived an impressive 10 minutes later. I chalked that up to my proximity to the university and hospital. Body parts in a yard can cause a bit of concern, especially if you're near either of those two places.

*****

My day was clearly getting off to the wrong start. Who the hell leaves a severed hand in someone's back yard? It's not like they tossed it over the fence. It was positioned so that I'd see it when I looked out the window, or opened the door. Shit, I haven't been back in Omaha long enough to have pissed off anybody but family. I mulled all this over as I ate breakfast. Yeah, I could still eat a little something.

Before heading out for a quick run, I wandered into my office to check messages. Blinking light. Good sign. My cash stash was getting a bit tight. I pressed play.

"Did you enjoy my gift?" *What the*? I pressed play, again.

"Did you enjoy my gift?" Definitely a man's voice. Older, maybe 40s or 50s. I felt my adrenaline kick into gear. I replayed the message two more times. Something about the voice was familiar.

The OPD was becoming my new BFF. They returned, and listened to the message a few times before starting in with the usual questions: Do you recognize the voice? Who do you think it might be? How long did you say you've been in Omaha? What did you do in NYC? The questions went on. They left saying they'd get back to me when they knew more.

After they left, Mike popped into my head. He couldn't possibly be that stupid, could he? How did he find me, anyway? There's no way him showing up in O'Malley's was a coincidence.

I decided he and I needed to have a chat. The problem was, I didn't know where he lived. Of course, humans are creatures of habit. So, I'd bet dollars to donuts, he was at Eddy's.

Eddy's was on the corner of 34th and Leavenworth. It was early, but this was the best lead I had. I saw Eddy behind the bar. His bald head sported an 8-ball on the back. It looked like he'd gained a little weight, but basically he was the same guy I met nine years ago. Tall, well-muscled, and flawless caramel-colored skin.

"Tangueray and tonic." I sat down. After a minute, he set the drink in front of me. He studied me, shook his head, and walked away. I looked around. The place was deserted.

"Dezeray Jackson!" He turned back and walked over, smiling wide. "Where the hell have you been? There hasn't been any decent hustlin' in here since … Shit! Since that night you and Mikey took down Ace and his partner. What was his name?"

"Duke." I smiled. "How've you been?"

"You know, same shit, different day. Where've you been hiding?"

"Here and there."

"When did ya get back?"

"Two months ago." I sipped my drink. "Listen, Eddy, I ran into Mike the other night. Any idea where I could find him?"

"Yeah, yeah. He's driving for some hotshot lawyer. Carmich, Carmichael … I don't know, something like that."

"Great, thanks." I put money down for my drink.

"It's on me. Glad you're back." He handed me the money, and I left with promises to return for a game or two.

Back in my car, I googled "Carmichael, and attorneys". Eddy was right. The office was located downtown in one of the renovated buildings off Dodge Street. I located it, and parked across the street a block down. My day was looking brighter. Mike was leaning next to a black Ford SUV, eating a sandwich.

Mike didn't notice me cross the street. I walked up behind the car and appeared next to him. Tapped his shoulder.

"Mikey."

He jumped. "Shit, Dez." A mouthful of food dribbled down the front of his shirt. "Goddamn it." He started wiping his shirt with his napkin.

"Why ya so jumpy, Mikey?" I smiled, and wiped a piece of lettuce from his chin.

"What the fuck do you want?"

"Now, no hard feelings. I mean, you surprised me the other night."

"Yeah, whatever."

I moved closer. "So, Mikey, what were you doing in O'Malley's? How'd you know I was back?"

"A mutual acquaintance may have mentioned it, that's all."

"Really? Who'd that be?"

"Look, Dez, I don't have time for your shit. I'm workin'." He crumbled up his wrappers and tossed them into a nearby can.

I leaned against the SUV. "Who you working for these days?"

"What the fuck do you care?"

"Just curious."

Mike rolled his eyes. "Jesus, woman. It's not what you think."

"Really?"

"Yeah, really. He's an attorney. Name's Carmichael."

I walked to the can to pitch my gum, and to get a look at the front of the SUV. The grill looked new.

"He's coming down for a meeting. You need to head out," Mike said.

I turned to face him. "How do you know Liz Gordan?"

"Who the fuck is that?"

"The woman you hit with this car the other night."

"I don't know any Liz Gordan."

A tall, well-dressed, tanned man approached the SUV.

"Time to go, Mike."

"Yes, sir." Mike pushed past me.

Carmichael smiled and opened the back door. He nodded his head. "Ms. Jackson." He got into the SUV.

Dumbfounded, I stood on the sidewalk and watched Mike pull away from the curb. How did Carmichael know my name? I didn't recognize him. The wind picked up. I put my hands in my pockets. The note. I forgot about the note. I pulled it out. It was a list of codes and names. I had no idea what any of it meant, but I knew someone who might. Back in my car, I called Tracer International.

"Haithem Nazari." His Arab-English accent was as strong as I remembered.

"Haithem! Dez Jackson. How are you?"

"Dez Jackson? Wow! It's been a few years, hasn't it?"

"Yes, yes, I know. I'm horrible about keeping in touch."

"Are you still in Florida?"

After college, I worked for Tracer for a year, then moved to Florida. I got stuck in Miami for five long years before lucking into the NYC gig. Truth was, I loved New York, but hated the job.

"No, no. I'm back in Omaha, actually."

"Oh, that's great! We should get together."

"That would be awesome. Listen, Haithem, I came across something that I was hoping you could help me figure out."

"Right. Always on the job," He laughed. "What is it?"

"Can I text a pic to you?"

He gave me his cellular number and we disconnected. About 10 minutes later, my phone rang.

"Dez, where'd you get this?"

"Someone handed it to me. Why?"

"From what I can tell, and this is just a cursory look, what you have here are security codes. In fact, they appear to be the type a bank might use for credit and debit cards. I can't explain the names."

"You mean like the three-digit code on the back?"

"Yep!"

"Thanks, Haithem. I'll be in touch."

Why did Ms. Gordan have these codes? Who was she?

My phone rang.

"Ms. Jackson. I believe you have something that belongs to my client." The voice. I knew that voice.

"I guess that depends. Who's your client?"

"That's not important. What I need you to do is give that list to Mike."

Carmichael.

"Oh, I don't know about that. I think I'll be a good citizen and hand it over to the OPD."

"That would be a mistake. Or, perhaps you didn't appreciate my gift?"

"Well, as gifts go, I'd have to say yours sucked."

"Meet Mike at O'Malley's in 20 minutes."

The phone disconnected. I could still take it to the police, but I couldn't explain the connection between Carmichael and Ms. Gordan. And, I couldn't prove that Carmichael left me that message. I also couldn't shake the feeling that I knew him from somewhere.

When I arrived, I saw Mike waiting near the front door of O'Malley's. I parked and walked a half block to reach him.

"Mike."

"Dez, where's the paper?"

"Oh, so now you know something about it?"

"I don't know nothin' he doesn't tell me. He tells me to get a list from you, and I get the list."

"Do you even know what it is?"

"I don't wanna know. Where's the list?"

"It's in my car."

"What the hell? Go get it!"

"Here's the thing. I'm not giving you the list. If Carmichael wants it, tell him to meet me at 62nd and Pine at eight o'clock." I walked back to my car.

I finally figured out why he seemed familiar.

*****

I drove to 62nd and Pine and parked. The temperature dropped about 10 degrees by 8 o'clock. I could swear I saw little snowflakes flitting in the air. It wasn't even the end of October, yet. The street was nearly empty. I walked over to the exact spot where Ms. Gordan died and scanned the area. That night, the SUV sped away, but it didn't go far. I recalled hearing it stop, but I was distracted by Ms. Gordan, and didn't see where it turned.

I returned to my car to wait for Carmichael. About 8:15, I saw his black SUV. He parked across the street from me. I waited for him to get out of his car, and then I stepped out.

"Bravo, Ms. Jackson." He walked toward me, clapping. "I see you've finally figured it out."

"But, why would she take a S.A.F.E class at the dojang you train in?"

"She came to me, after discovering what her employer was doing. She confided in me."

"You set her up."

"Guilty as charged." He walked closer to me. "Ms. Gordan proved to be a liability. One my client and I simply couldn't afford."

"And the bruising on her arms?"

"That was Zack, I'm afraid. Ms. Gordan confronted him. He lost control."

"She said someone was back. Who was she talking about?" I moved closer to the sidewalk.

"Again, guilty."

"You were following her — trying to scare her."

"Right, again."

He was within arm's reach. I backed up onto the sidewalk.

"Give me the list?"

"Oh, about that. I'd love to help you out there, but I gave it to the OPD."

He reached for me. I blocked left and grabbed his wrist. My punch landed on his jaw. I stepped into him, wrapped my arm around his waist, and flipped him. I kept hold of his left wrist, locked his arm, stepped over him, and kept twisting. Sirens blared, or maybe it was him crying. Either way, my new BFF had arrived. I'd phoned them on my way to meet Carmichael. Always have backup. That's rule number two.

*****

For days, my phone wouldn't stop ringing. Every beat reporter in the city wanted to talk to me. In the end, I gave an exclusive to WOWT, the local NBC affiliate. I like their style. And, you never know, it could lead to a spot with Matt Lauer on The Today Show.

Carmichael, and Zach Thomas, the owner of Secure Tech, were arrested for conspiracy to commit murder, murder, fraud, and a whole host of other stuff. What a waste.

I took Haithem up on his invitation to get together. We met for drinks at Eddy's. He wasn't much of a shooter. Mike showed up. He kept his distance, but I knew he was watching my game. I'd have to school him again, but not tonight. Tonight was all about having a good time.

CHAPTER FOUR

DUPING DELIGHT

The crunch of gravel under my tires faded as I slid to a stop at a crossroad. Farmland surrounded me. I was out of my element and my GPS knew it. Directions stopped two miles back when I was still on a paved road. I rummaged through the file on the passenger seat for the address I had scribbled on a post-it. County Road 236. Where the hell was it? And, why don't they have signs out here? I looked left, and then right. Corn blocked my view. I eased the car forward and looked left, again. There was a woman walking away from me down the road. I turned and approached the woman.

I rolled down my window. "Excuse me."

The woman continued walking.

"I wonder if you could tell me what road this is?"

"Go just down there." The woman pointed in the distance without looking at me. "You're nearly there, Ms. Jackson." Her words were slow and revealed a southern twang.

My foot hit the brake. The car slid on the gravel. My file flew to the floor. The woman continued walking. Her long dress swayed with the methodical movement of her hips. She stepped off of the road into the ditch and disappeared into a cornfield.

"What the?" I muttered, searching the side of the road. "All right, then. You got my attention."

I followed the road to a dead end. A tree-lined driveway appeared on my right. "Isn't this lovely."

The driveway stretched on for a quarter mile. A large, dilapidated farmhouse appeared. I parked my Jeep underneath the shade branches of a large Mulberry tree and got out. The steps creaked as I climbed to the porch, which slanted to the right. I searched for a doorbell. It hung from frayed wire. I opened the screen door and knocked on the wood door. The sound of feet shuffling across a floor grew louder. The door opened.

"But, how?" It was the woman I'd seen on the road. I looked behind me and then back at her.

The old woman's almost toothless grin sent a shiver down my spine.

"Won't you come in? It's a bit too cool outside for my tastes."

I followed the woman into a sparsely-appointed living room.

"May I offer you some lemonade?"

I nodded.

"Please, do sit down." She poured lemonade from a glass pitcher into tumblers on a nearby table. "Cookies?"

She handed me the lemonade and sat down. She gestured to a plate.

"No, thank you."

I put Mayville Toussaint at about 72 years old. Her long, gray hair was pulled back and twisted into a braid that she wrapped around her head. She was from some place near Savannah, GA, and had relocated to Nebraska several months ago. I didn't know why. I decided to get right to the point.

"Your letter stated that something was stolen from you."

"Yes."

"What was it?"

"A box."

"A box?"

"Yes."

"What kind of box?"

She handed me a picture. The box was about six inches long and four inches wide. It was hand-carved.

"What are these symbols?"

"You needn't concern yourself with them."

"Is there anything in the box?"

"Yes."

"Care to tell me what?"

"No."

"When was the box stolen?"

"Several months back while I was in Savannah. The people who stole it came to Nebraska."

"How do you know?"

"I know."

"Ms. Toussaint, if I'm going to help you, you're going to need to trust me."

She smiled. "Find the box and return it to me before the full moon. That's in one week." She slid an envelope across the table. "This is all you need to know."

I opened the envelope. It included my initial payment of $5000, two names — Ramey Barrows and Holt Landry — their pictures and addresses.

"If you know where they are, why not go to the police? File a report?"

"It's not the sort of thing the police can handle."

I stood to leave. Ms. Toussaint walked me to the door and opened it, allowing me to pass in front of her.

"And, Ms. Jackson, you're going to want to open that box."

I turned to look at her. Her deep blue eyes stared at me through small, round-rimmed glasses. She was about 5 feet tall and held a wood-handled cane in her left hand. I didn't remember seeing it before.

"I'm warning you, now. Don't open the box."

*****

Ramey Barrows lived in a condo in midtown Omaha. Judging from his picture, I wasn't sure how he could afford the place. I pressed the elevator button for the 10th floor. It stopped once on the way up. Two upwardly mobile twenty-somethings entered chattering about the latest gadget they'd bought. I was clearly in the wrong occupation. They exited on the 9th floor. I exhaled. I was certain I had lost IQ points listening to their textspeak.

Barrows' condo was near the end of the west corridor. I rang the bell. About a minute passed. I rang the bell, again. It was a long shot. He was probably working. I turned to walk back to the elevator. A tall, tanned well-built guy with a neatly trimmed goatee passed me. I stopped and turned around. I'll be damned. He cleaned up nicely. I hurried to catch up with him.

"Excuse me?" I asked.

He stopped just before reaching his door and turned around. His eyes were dark like chocolate. Wow. Snap out of it, Jackson. His smile revealed bright white teeth and a slight dimple in his right cheek. I gulped. He was GQ material.

"Yes?"

"Hi, are you Ramey Barrows?"

"Yes, ma'am. And, who might you be?"

"Dezeray Jackson."

"Oh, a southerner like myself! Pleased to meet you, Ms. Jackson." He held out his hand.

"Not exactly. At least, not for a few generations." I smiled as he accepted my hand and kissed it. That was unexpected.

"Mr. Barrows, if you have a few minutes, I'd like to talk with you about this." I removed the picture of the box from the folder in my bag. His brow furrowed as he studied it.

"Do you recognize the box?" I asked.

"No, I surely don't. It is beautiful." His hand caressed the image.

"Are you certain? I was told that you would be the person to ask."

He handed me the picture.

"I'm terribly sorry, Ms. Jackson, but I'm afraid I can't help you. Now, if you'll excuse me, I have an appointment for which I mustn't be late." He nodded, smiled, and continued to his condo.

I watched as he walked away. His suit wasn't off the rack. I'd noticed his tie, too. Savile Row. Where'd he get his money? I shoved the picture into my bag and headed back to the elevator. My car was parked at a meter on the street just outside the parking garage. I decided to wait for him.

Ten minutes later, a red Porsche Boxster eased through the security gate. It was Barrows. Luck was on my side today and it wasn't even St. Patrick's Day. I kept a few cars between us as I followed him downtown. He got to 24th and Leavenworth Streets and parked in a lot. I did the same, and watched as he crossed the street. He entered the 11 Worth Cafe. Nice. I could eat a little something. My stomach rumbled its agreement.

The place was busy. Lunch rush. I found a spot at the counter where I could see Barrows, but he couldn't see me. He sat in a booth across from a man with salt and pepper hair trimmed short in back, but longer in the front. A day's worth of stubble covered his face. His shirt was too large for his frame and his jeans had holes in the knees. He seemed familiar.

I grabbed my bag from the floor and searched for the picture of the other guy Mayville Toussaint wanted me to find. There was a resemblance, but the guy in my picture had short brown hair. He was clean shaven and dressed in a three-piece tailored suit. Still, it might be him. If it was, I couldn't help but wonder what the hell had happened to him.

Barrows handed the other man an envelope. The man didn't open it. He tucked it into his jacket pocket, took a bite of his sandwich, and left. I paid my bill and followed him.

*****

The man sauntered east toward downtown. I watched him for a while. A block away, he got into a beat up Chevy truck. I eased from the parking lot and followed as he turned south. He turned east to 13th street and south again. After about 15 minutes, he pulled over and parked outside a bar.

I waited in my Jeep, debating the wiseness of entering a dive bar at 1:30 in the afternoon in South Omaha. Entertaining as it might be, I wasn't sure I was in the mood. By 2 o'clock, I was bored.

The place was dimly lit, as expected. Several men lined the bar. None so much as glanced in my direction when the door opened allowing in some much-needed fresh air. My eyes adjusted. There were a few pool tables — coin-operated, an old jukebox in a corner playing salsa music, a few tables scattered around and five booths. My guy was seated at the booth farthest from the door. A Hispanic woman tended bar while another one cleaned tables.

I ordered a gin and tonic and set it on a table near my mark.

"You shoot?" I asked.

"Some."

"Feel like shootin'?"

"Why not. Ain't doin' much else at the present time." He stood and towered over me, his southern accent somewhat mellow, but evident. He set his drink, whiskey, if I had to hazard a guess, on his table on top of a piece of paper. A crumbled envelope sat next to the salt and pepper shakers.

"You break," I said.

He moved to the head of the table as I set the rack.

"Straight, bank the 8, ball in hand?" I asked.

"Sounds like you know your way around a table."

"Some."

He smiled and nodded.

We played without much chatter and I let him run the table. He'd downed two shots of scotch - Johnnie Walker Black - before our game ended. My drink sat on the table, untouched.

"Looks like you lose," his southern draw more pronounced.

"Yeah, looks like. How about another go?"

"Rack'em, little girl."

I took a deep breath. Beating him down was counter-productive.

"So, where ya from?" I asked.

"Georgia. You?"

I got that a lot. My accent was all over the map.

"Here and there. Lately, more here than there." I grinned. He smiled. Nice smile. "What brings you to the heartland?"

"Family."

Smack! The balls flew across the table. The high yellow ball fell, along with the low red. He went for highs. Missed.

"That's a good thing, I hope," I said, and took low balls.

"Thought it was at the time." He walked around the table, studying the layout. "15 left corner." He jammed the cue ball behind a low ball with no way out. "Your ball."

I picked it up. "How long you been in town?" I walked around the table for my next shot.

"'Bout six months too long." He stopped at his table and downed another shot. He signaled to the bartender for another round.

"Omaha isn't that bad. The zoo is amazing."

That got a chuckle. "Suppose yer right 'bout that." He set down his stick to pay for his drink. "Sorry, did you want anything?"

"No, I'm good. Thanks."

The waitress picked up the money and returned to cleaning.

"So, what's your story?" he asked.

Bingo.

"Not much to tell, really. I came across something interesting and I'm just checkin' it out."

"What's that?"

"How can I be sure I can trust you?" I smiled one of those super-sweet flirty smiles and batted my eyes a bit.

He moved within arm's reach. The mixed aroma of scotch and nachos nearly knocked me out. He leaned and whispered into my ear.

"I'm very trustworthy." His lips grazed my cheek as he pulled away. If it hadn't been for the pungent scotch-and-nachos smell, and the fact that this was a job, I might have let this play out.

I sighed. "Perhaps, but a girl's gotta be careful, ya know." I moved away and took aim at the 3-ball.

"Now you got me real curious."

I looked at him over my shoulder. He was staring at my ass.

"Your shot." I stood and moved my drink to his table.

"So, you gonna tell me your secret?" he asked, as he smacked the 14-ball into the side. "Maybe I can help you check it out." The rugged southern thing was working for him. His blue jeans fit just right. He'd taken off the over-size shirt, showing off a beautifully-sculpted torso. And, the piece de resistance — brown, leather, pointy cowboy boots. *Oy.*

I retrieved the picture of the box from my bag. "This is supposed to be something really special. Problem is, the guy I was told to see says he doesn't know anything about it."

He took the paper from my hand and studied the picture.

"Where'd you get this?" he asked.

"Some old man. Said he'd pay me good if I could get my hands on it."

He handed the paper back.

"Yer wastin' your time."

"What are you talkin' about? That old man seemed pretty sure. What do you know about it, anyway?"

He scoffed and finished another shot. "I know plenty."

*****

After several hours with Holt Landry, he told me Ramey Barrows had the box, and kept it with him. Odd, but okay. Landry explained how he could help me get my hands on the box.

"Why are you so willing to help me out?" I asked.

"We can split the take. Way I see it, you can't get the box without me and Barrows doesn't exactly trust me."

"So how do you see this goin' down?" I asked.

"Barrows ain't nothin' more than a con. For the right price, he'd give up the box."

"The right price? How much?"

"Half a mil."

"For the box? You're shittin' me. It's a wood box for Christ's sake, not the Crown jewels."

"You don't know much about that box, do ya?"

No, as a matter of fact, I didn't know squat about it, but he didn't need confirmation of that.

"I know it's got to be worth at least $100 thousand, easy."

He shook his head, downed another shot and chased it with a beer.

"All ya have ta do is make Barrows believe ya got the money. I know a guy who can get his hands on what we need."

Landry gave me his number and I left him in the bar. It was time to reach out to Barrows again. Back in my Jeep I found his address and made a call to my former colleague, Haithem Nazari. He picked up on the first ring.

"Hi, Haithem. It's Dez."

"Ah, Dez, how are you this fine evening? I wondered when I'd hear from you, again. We still need to have that dinner you promised me."

A month ago, Haithem helped me out on a case on the condition that I let him take me to dinner. Normally, I wouldn't pass up an opportunity to eat out on someone else's dime, but this was different.

"Oh, yeah! You know, I've been crazy busy. We'll get together, soon. Really."

"But?"

"But right now, I need you to get me a number for a guy named Ramey Barrows." I gave Barrow's address.

"Give me a minute." He put me on hold. While I waited, I searched my console for a snack. All that talk about dinner made me hungry. I made a mental note to stop at the store on the way home to grab some sushi. Godfrey, my Rottie, was out of food, too, and not patient about missing meals.

"Okay, here it is." Haithem gave me the number. I thanked him and promised to get back in touch next week.

I didn't see Landry exit the bar, but his truck was gone. That wasn't good, considering how many shots he'd had. I dialed Ramey Barrows' number. He picked up on the third ring. I put him on speaker phone to keep my hands free.

"Mr. Barrows, this is Dezeray Jackson. We met earlier today."

"Yes, Ms. Jackson, I remember. And, it seems you've tracked me down again."

"If you have time, I'd like to meet with you tomorrow about the box."

"I told you I don't know anything about that box."

"Yes, I know that's what you said, but my collector assures me that you do, and he's willing to pay you a considerable finder's fee."

Silence. I was surprised it was taking him so long to think it over.

"A finder's fee? And how much might that be?"

"I'm not at liberty to discuss it in detail right now. How about we get together tomorrow afternoon?"

"Well, I certainly can't turn down a request from a beautiful lady such as yourself. Where would you like to meet?"

"How about Elmwood Park Grotto at 2 o'clock?"

"I'll see you then."

The line disconnected.

*****

Holt Landry met up with me at 1:30 p.m., in a lot on the south side of Elmwood Park, for the drop off. I didn't ask where he got the money. Plausible deniability. He handed me an army- green duffel bag.

"We'll meet back here at 2:30 p.m.," he said. He was looking pretty good for a guy who had at least six shots of Johnnie Walker Black the night before.

I nodded, walked back to my Jeep, and tossed the bag onto the passenger seat.

Elmwood Park is located on the far west boundary of midtown Omaha. It's a sprawling 200-acre park on the backside of the University of Nebraska-Omaha. During spring and summer, it's filled with people throughout the day. In fall, it's a little less crowded, and The Grotto is a cozy semiprivate spot. I parked in the lot adjacent to the path leading to The Grotto. Barrow's car wasn't around. I checked the time. He still had about five minutes. I grabbed the money bag, got out, walked down the stone steps leading to The Grotto and waited near the rock fountains.

A short time later, I heard footsteps. Ramey Barrows approached The Grotto, carrying a brown leather satchel. His overcoat billowed behind him. He met me at the fountain.

"Ms. Jackson, you're looking as lovely as the day before. My eyes would never tire of seeing you." He smiled. Heat rose up my neck. My face felt hot. Dimple. Wow. Focus, Jackson. Geez.

"Who is your collector friend?"

"I'm not at liberty to say. Do you have the box?"

"So quick to conclude our business." He set his bag on a rock ledge and opened it. The box rested inside. "May I?" He reached for the duffel bag. I removed the box from the satchel and then handed him the bag.

"I'll take that." Landry appeared seemingly out of nowhere with a gun pointed at us. I hate guns pointed at me. It really pisses me off. I turned to face him.

Barrows dropped the bag and held his hands in front of him. "Come on now, Holt, we don't need to get violent. I'm sure we can work something out."

"I got everything worked out, Ramey, don't you worry 'bout that. Now, scoot that bag over this way."

Ramey Barrows gave the bag a small push.

"Don't test me," Landry said.

Barrows kicked it harder. It landed in front of Landry.

"You!" He directed his attention to me. "Bring me the box."

I walked to him and handed him the box. My gaze moved from the gun to his eyes. A bead of sweat covered his upper lip.

"I'll be getting that back from you before the day ends."

"Back off or you'll be bleeding in the next thirty seconds."

I took a few steps back. The gun, in the small of my back under my jacket, shifted. The corner of Landry's mouth twitched as he watched me. I kept my hands low at my sides and in view. I could drop him. He was off. Not a shooter. I heard gravel scrape the ground. Barrows ran for the steps. Landry let him go. Keeping his eyes on me and the gun pointed at my stomach, he leaned down, and set the box inside the bag. He closed it, stood, and flung the duffel over his shoulder.

"Don't follow me," he said.

"Don't need to."

I watched Landry disappear through the trees.

*****

I got back into my Jeep and turned on my tablet. Landry's car blipped onto my screen. My former employer had given a few Spark Nano 4.0 GPS trackers to me, but I'd never gotten around to returning them before I left Florida. Good thing!

Landry was in North Omaha near 16th and Locust streets. I headed in that direction. He was probably meeting up with Clive Dixon. That was the name on the paper in the envelope. I'd run a check on Dixon the night before. Now I was committed to dinner and a movie with Haithem, but at least I knew who I was dealing with. Clive Dixon was a low-level con until recently.

I followed Dodge to 24th and Cuming Streets and then drove north to Locust. 24th Street used to have nothing but housing projects, run-down buildings, and broken-down people. The projects were replaced with reasonable single-family homes and strip malls. A few national-brand businesses had opened, creating much-needed jobs. One staple remained — Skeets Barbecue. It'd been years since I tasted their ribs and chicken. I pulled over, ordered my food, and hopped back into my Jeep. The aroma of their sauce sent my mind back to when I was a kid. My father loved their ribs and chicken. He'd bring us all the way from our place clear out west just to get some. Back then, the buildings were always dark and scary. Now, the streets were well-lit. As I passed Love's Jazz & Art Center, I remembered that a few people told me I should check it out. Maybe I'd take Haithem there on our date. There aren't any movies worth seeing right now anyway. My stomach grumbled, and my mind told it to shut up and wait.

At Locust Street, I turned east to 16th. Most of the houses were large, old, single-family homes followed by stretches of undeveloped land, with the exception of a housing development I didn't know existed. Just past that, though, were several old commercial buildings. Some were occupied by legitimate businesses, but Clive Dixon's business didn't fall into that category. A month or so ago, he got into moving counterfeit money.

I spotted Landry's truck and turned south, away from it. Halfway down the road, I made a U-turn so I could park a few blocks away and keep an eye on his truck. It was three o'clock. I looked around. Not a lot happening this time of day. The Chubb Foods' parking lot was virtually empty. No one was walking around. I decided to take a walk up the block to Landry's truck. Maybe he left the box inside.

Sure enough it was right on the front seat. I could just make it out under his jacket. I checked the door. Unlocked. Idiot. I eased the door open, reached under the jacket, and grabbed the box. Before hightailing it back to my Jeep, I arranged his jacket so that it looked like the box was still there.

As I turned left onto Locust, Landry came out from one of the old buildings. He saw me.

"You bitch!" He ran into the middle of the street. I didn't bother stopping, but did manage to smile and wave with a drumstick in my hand.

Just in case he got the bright idea to follow me, I turned right off Locust, headed north to Florence, and then jumped on the North Freeway at Ames Street. I made my way through light traffic to I-80 and followed it out of Omaha. My GPS showed Landry on the move, but he wasn't following me. Ms. Toussaint would have her box by nightfall.

I still didn't understand what was so special about the old box or why Barrows and Landry stole it in the first place. There didn't seem to be anything inside it any of the times I held it. What would someone want with an empty wood box? Yeah, it was hand-carved, but it couldn't be worth much. I thought about it all the way to Ms. Toussaint's place.

When I arrived at her house, something seemed off. I couldn't put my finger on it. I retrieved my gun from under the seat before getting out and put it in my holster. Dusk in the country. Creepy. I approached the front door. It was open.

"Ms. Toussaint?" I entered the main hall. The house was quiet except for the sound of something — dripping? What the hell is dripping? As I walked the hall in search of the noise and Ms. Toussaint, I looked in the living room. Empty. I figured the kitchen was in the back of the house. The stairs leading to the second floor were past the living room. Water was trickling down each step and a pool of water formed at the bottom. I climbed the stairs and located what I believed was the bathroom. The door was closed, but not locked. I turned the knob and pushed the door open. In the center of the room was a claw-foot tub overflowing with water. I moved closer. Barrows' lifeless eyes looked up at me from the tub.

Retracing my steps, I returned to the main floor. Where was Ms. Toussaint? I found the kitchen. Empty. The back door was open. I stepped outside. There was a path leading away from the house. I could make out a faint light. Gun in hand, I walked the path. After a short distance, I stumbled over something. I looked down expecting to see a meandering tree root. It was a leg.

I bent down to inspect the body. The boot looked familiar. Most of it was covered in leaves and the head was under a row of low-growing evergreens. Landry. No pulse. How the hell did he get here? How did either of them know where Ms. Toussaint was?

The faint light in the distance flickered. I stepped over Landry's leg and kept walking. The path led to a small makeshift shed. A light hung on the outside, moving each time there was a breeze. I heard singing, or maybe it was chanting.

"Come in, Ms. Jackson. Do you have my box?"

I holstered my gun and pulled open the wood screen door. The room was crowded with jars containing with things I couldn't quite make out. Several dead chickens hung from the ceiling. A pile of what looked like bones rested on a crate in a corner.

"My box, Ms. Jackson. Where is it?"

"My Jeep. It's in my Jeep."

"Good. Leave it on the table in the hall before you go."

"Ms. Toussaint, how did Barrows and Landry get here?"

Her back was to me. She seemed to be stirring something in a large pot.

"Don't know who yer talkin' 'bout."

"Landry is on the trail and Barrows is in your bathroom."

"I think you might be mistaken."

"Ms. Toussaint, I didn't imagine their bodies."

"The eyes can play tricks on us." She turned to face me. Her eyes, completely white, changed back to the deep blue I had seen the day we met.

"Did you have someone kill them?"

"No one killed anybody, Ms. Jackson. Sometimes people just get their due. Lustin' after things can have that effect on a body."

"Why'd they steal your box?"

"I just told you."

"Lusting? After what?"

"Money, power, fame — the usual."

"What's in the box, Ms. Toussaint?"

"Nothing that would concern you, Ms. Jackson. Just leave the box on the hall table. And don't forget the rest of your fee. It's in an envelope on the table."

She turned back to cleaning a boning knife. A few seconds later, she began to hum a tune. It slowly became a chant. I stared at her back, and started to move forward to touch her shoulder. Something told me not to. Something told me that Ms. Toussaint was crazy. Time to go. I turned and stepped out into the night.

The door slammed against the frame behind me. I took my penlight out of my back pocket. I didn't want to trip over Landry.

As I hurried to the house, I could hear Ms. Toussaint; her chanting was growing louder. I dashed through the house to my Jeep, and grabbed the box off of the passenger seat. I turned to the house; Ms. Toussaint's chanting continued to get louder. I headed for the door, then stopped.

"Jesus, Dez. Get a grip. There are two dead bodies. You need to report this," I whispered to myself.

I grabbed my cell to take pictures. I ran to the base of the stairs, stood transfixed. I looked down. There wasn't any water. The stairs were dry. I climbed the steps two at a time and threw the bathroom door open. No Barrows. I ran down the stairs, through the kitchen and back to the trail. I searched the spot where I knew I'd seen Landry. There was nothing but an old tree log crossing the trail. I stepped over it and ran to the shed at the end of the trail. No shed. I grabbed my gun and strained to see if there was anything or anyone in the field. An owl hooted somewhere high up in a tree. A dog barked. I turned and ran back to the house. The kitchen door clattered against the door frame as I rushed inside. I went to the hall table. No box.

I ran to my Jeep, set my gun and the envelope on the console. I took a few deep breaths to slow my breathing. I stared into the darkness, and tried to make sense of what had happened. I couldn't. Maybe part of me didn't want to. I started the Jeep and sped away as fast as I could.

Later that night, I opened the envelope from Ms. Toussaint. I wanted to be certain the money was there. It was.

So was a note. It read: Be careful what YOU lust after, Ms. Jackson. Until we meet, again.

CHAPTER FIVE

MURPHY

"Dammit!" I scanned for oncoming cars, then stepped off of the curb and crouched to get a better look. "Christ, where is it?" I reached into my jacket pocket for my penlight. "There you are you little bugger." My car key balanced on a small lip just inside the sewer drain. I checked for cars, again.

"Watcha doin' there, lady?"

I looked up to see a raggedy-looking guy peering down at me. His well-tanned face was hidden by a baseball cap and sunglasses.

"I dropped something." I returned my attention to the task at hand. I reached through the hole.

"Watch out!" The man grabbed my jacket and yanked me onto the sidewalk as a truck sped past.

Catching my breath, I said, "Thanks." I stood and brushed dust off my butt and legs.

"No problem. Let me see if I can get it." He laid down on the sidewalk with his head just over the edge. "Give me the light." He reached his hand behind him, fingers wiggling.

I handed it to him and kept a lookout for more dumb-ass, crazy drivers.

"Almost got it! Oh, crap!"

"What?" I stepped from the curb and struggled to see.

"Rats! I hate rats." He popped up and jumped to his feet. "Here you go."

"Thanks." I started rummaging in my leather backpack for a few bucks. "Let me give you a little something."

He smiled.

"Nah, don't worry about it. I'm good."

"Seriously, let me at least buy you a coffee or something."

"Awright, tea. I could use some tea. And, maybe a pastry."

Eyebrow raised, I said, "Okay. Tea it is."

We walked in silence about half a block to the 11th-Worth Cafe. The breakfast crowd was gone, and it was too early for lunch. We took a booth near the windows.

"Name's Murphy."

"Dezeray Jackson."

"Aren't you that PI that was in the news recently?"

I nodded. He was referring to a hit-and-run case I'd solved a few months back.

"That Carmichael guy was a real dick. Got what he deserved, if you ask me."

The waitress brought us his tea and a roll. She set a glass of water in front of me.

"Did you know him?" I asked.

"Yeah. Not a giver, that one."

I shook my head in agreement. "So, what's your story?"

"Not much to tell."

"You pulled me out of the way of that truck like it was nothin.'"

He chuckled at that. "I like to stay active."

I noticed his watch. G-Shock G110.

"How long were you in?"

He took a bite of his roll. "I did a few tours."

His beard touched the tip of his T-shirt. The wavy, dark hair beneath his baseball cap reached his shoulders.

"You from Omaha?" I asked.

"Yeah. Grew up here. Graduated from Creighton Prep."

The expression on my face gave away my surprise.

"That hard to believe, huh?" he asked.

"Well, yeah, actually."

Creighton Prep was a single-sex Catholic boys' college-prep school. Most of the kids came from families who had money. Sure, there were exceptions -- like, apparently, this guy.

"I had a scholarship."

"How long you been back?"

"A few months. I'm looking for someone."

"Maybe I can help."

He finished his roll and added more hot water to his tea bag.

"Don't think so."

"Why's that?"

"I already found her."

He took off his sunglasses and looked me in the eye. Crows-feet stretched out from his bright blue eyes.

There are no coincidences in life. I leaned back. My hands rested on the edge of the table. I took a deep breath.

"It's been a longtime," I said.

"Yeah. Too long."

Murphy had been living in a cheap motel across the river since he got discharged. Last I saw him was outside The Diner downtown. It was raining and cold. He had enlisted in the

Marines earlier that day. We'd dated since sophomore year. I was pissed when he left and never answered his letters, but they didn't stop coming until my last year at University of Nebraska-Lincoln.

"I've seen a lot of shit, Dez. In the beginning, all I had were memories of you. It got me through."

"Why'd you come back?" I asked.

"I had to. Things aren't settled."

I shifted in my seat. "Look, that's all in the past. And, I don't have time for it." I stood to leave. He reached for my hand. Man, he was quick.

"Hear me out, then go if you want."

I sat back down.

He explained that his brother was murdered two months ago. Now, I felt like a shit. I thought this was about us. When Murphy got discharged, he headed for Omaha to find me.

"I want you to find out who killed my brother."

I sat with Murphy for a few hours getting the details, avoiding the personal catching-up crap that can make your brain turn to mush. Lucky for me, he was relatively focused. Definitely not the kid I knew back in the day.

"I'll check into it, see if anything surfaces," I said.

"Sounds, good. And, Dez?"

Our eyes met.

"Thanks."

"Well, I haven't done anything, yet." I stood and left.

*****

Traffic was light. I made my way over to Eddy's. If anyone knew anything about what went down in North Omaha, it'd be Eddy.

The place was empty, but pretty soon the after-work crowd would march through the door. I sat down at the bar, with a line of sight to the door.

"Dez! How's it goin' girl?"

"Same shit, different day. You?"

"You know. What can I get ya?"

"Gin and tonic. Thanks, Eddy." He wiped down the bar space in front of me before moving away to make my drink. A minute later, he set it in front of me. "Pretzels?" He gestured to a bowl a few feet from me. *Yuck.*

"No, thanks. Hey, Eddy? You ever hear of a guy by the name of Paul Murphy?"

He wiped his hands on a bar towel, then said, "Ya know somethin,' that name rings a bell." He walked away to take another order. I scanned the hall. Slim pickin' so far.

Eddy returned. "Now, I know who he is. That's the guy was killed a few months back. Officially, it was an accident. Least, that's how it was reported."

"So, what's the unofficial word?"

Eddy leaned closer, resting his elbows on the bar, with his fingers laced in front of him. "Unofficially? There's rumors."

"What kind of rumors?"

"Some say it was a cop that did it. Some say the dude was in the wrong place, at the wrong time. Most people say it was a drug thing." He stepped away to grab a glass of water from behind him.

"What do you think?"

He looked back. "Me? What I think 'bout some white dude gettin' offed? Doesn't much matter in my world."

"Let's say it was a drug thing. If someone was interested in maybe finding a bit more detail, where would that someone go?"

"Girl, you been away too long. You know where the big dogs roll, and it ain't in North O."

"You're not sayin'?"

"You know exactly what I'm tellin' you.

I thanked Eddy for the info and the drink -- he always paid for the first one. The crowd was picking up, and I saw a few marks, but I didn't have time. *Damn.*

It was Friday night. I hopped into my Jeep and checked myself in the mirror. Not a good look. I drove home to glam up. Godfrey, my Rottie, met me at the door. I followed him to the kitchen and filled his bowl before heading to my room for a wardrobe change. Fifteen minutes later, I was out the door and back in my Jeep. Easy Street was downtown. My former colleague, Haitham Nazari, made sure I was on the list. It was time to see how the other half got their groove on.

*****

I drove east on Douglas Street and turned north on 10th street. A small crowd gathered on the corner of 10th and Dodge streets, just outside the club. I turned west and parked in a garage. As I walked closer, I saw the red ropes keeping the already overpopulated line under control. I walked around the throng of people to the front.

A muscle-bound, bald-headed, six-foot bouncer wearing a black suit and dark glasses looked down at me. I smiled.

"Dezeray Jackson. I believe my name is on your list." I pointed to a small clipboard in his large hand.

He scanned it, nodded to an equally imposing man to his left, and I was ushered past the red-velvet rope. Ah, it's good to have influential friends, or in this case, friends who can manipulate a guest list through hacking.

Eddy told me that the person I was looking for was usually on the second level, near the back. Getting through the crowd was like getting on a New York subway during rush hour. I finally found the stairs. The upper level encircled the dance floor and stage on the main level, allowing patrons to watch their prey.

I ordered a gin and tonic to blend in better. The guy next to me at the bar decided to strike up a conversation.

"My name's Rick, can I get that for you?"

I glanced in his direction, then looked back at the bartender who'd just delivered my drink.

"Oh, that's really sweet of you, but I've got this one. Thanks."

Rick placed a twenty on the bar. "Really, I insist. Beautiful women should never have to pay for their own drinks."

The bartender started to reach for the twenty. I set my hand on his and shook my head. I handed him a ten, grabbed my drink, and turned to leave. Rick followed.

Placing his hand on my shoulder, he asked, "How about a dance? You look amazing in that dress. Be a shame not to show it off on the dance floor."

I was wearing my little black dress with sequence around the hem line. Every woman has that "go-to"_dress, and this was mine. I turned to face him. His bright white teeth blinded me. Good-looking guy, stupid as fuck. "I appreciate that. Really, I do, but I'm waiting for someone." Not a complete lie. I turned to leave. His hand was on my shoulder, again. I reached up, squeezed his fingers together, careful to apply pressure between his thumb and pointer finger, and waited.

"Okay, okay. Sorry."

I let go and continued walking. The VIP section was a few yards away.

A red-velvet rope separated the VIPs from the average folk. Another bouncer guarded the section. In the center, seated on a couch, was the person I needed to see. Haithem was able to get me on the list, but not into the VIP section. That, I had to do on my own.

I left my drink on a table as I approached the rope.

"Pass?"

"Oh, sorry, let me find it." I searched through my small, black bag. It held two throwing stars, my phone, lipstick, ID, cash, and my counterfeit VIP pass. These places were all the same. I showed the bouncer, he unclipped the rope, and let me pass.

I stopped at a rectangular stone table in front of the couch.

"You got a minute?" I asked.

"Dezeray Jackson? Well, well. It's about time you came to see me. Heard you were back." The woman shifted her position to better see me. She waved at a man seated in a chair next to the couch. He stood. "Please, join me." She told her followers to leave, except the man. "You ready to accept my offer?"

Once upon a time, Katrina recruited me as part of her security team. Problem was, I didn't like the idea of working the wrong side of the law. Shades of gray, I can live with, but out-right lawbreaking didn't work for me.

"Not, yet. I just have a question, and I was hoping you might be able to give me some insight."

"You know that I don't discuss business outside of the family."

"I know, but I was hoping you might make an exception."

"What's in it for me?" She leaned forward to get her wine glass.

"Katrina, come on."

"Dez, you want something from me, and I want something from you. Information isn't free. How about this, I'll help you out, if I can, and you owe me a favor to be repaid at my leisure."

"Fine, but the usual parameters apply."

Katrina smiled. She was flawless. Most men stumbled over themselves the minute she entered a room. Women wanted to be her. She was tall and thin like a runway model. Her long, straight blonde hair was pushed to one side and fell in front of her shoulder. When we were young, I envied her, but time has a funny way of changing one's perspective. And, I knew most of her secrets.

I pulled out my phone and showed her a picture of Paul Murphy.

"Do you remember him?" I asked.

"That was a bad situation."

"So, you know who he is?"

"Dez, it was all over the news. Of course, I know who he is."

"Katrina, this is Patrick Murphy's brother."

Her eyes lit up as she remembered Patrick. "I never made the connection when it happened."

"Was his brother into drugs?"

"No. Not even back then."

"How can you be sure?"

"If my people had any connection to that incident, I would know."

Katrina controlled the entire drug scene in Omaha. She orchestrated the buys and distribution. Anyone working for her, and every major dealer was, understood how she handled disloyalty to the family. She was fine with little skirmishes among underlings. She believed they weeded out the weaker employees. If some regular white guy got offed by someone in her ranks, she'd make damn sure there was a good reason. And, in most of those cases, she would have ordered the hit.

"Thanks." I stood to leave.

"Remember our agreement, Dez."

*****

The next day, I spent the morning reviewing the police reports. All of the reports indicated that Paul's body was found in a ditch near a series of old, abandoned buildings. The investigating officers didn't find any evidence at the scene, trace or otherwise, that explained who strangled him. They knew that the body was dumped in the ditch. The officer, who originally discovered Paul's body, was off duty. In his report, he stated that he'd been working in the area providing security for a business that recently opened.

I flipped through the last report and I saw a name I recognized -- Clive Dixon. He was a low-level smuggler, but didn't deal in drugs. His thing was counterfeit paper, forgery, and artwork. The off-duty officer found Dixon near the scene and detained him, but the police didn't have evidence linking him to the murder. They had to let him go.

No one was working the case day to day. Cold case, plain and simple. Murphy was right about that part, but I was curious about the coroner's report. It stated that the cause of death was asphyxiation and that the body had been wiped clean. Who knows how to do that? That's got to be a pretty short list. I closed the files.

My phone rang. I hit the speaker phone button.

"Dezeray Jackson Investigations. This is Dez."

"Ms. Jackson, You really should be more careful."

The line went dead.

Godfrey was barking. I left my office and found him, nose to the ground, at the front door. Smoke. I smelled smoke. I grabbed the phone from the coffee table, dialed 911, and went to the bay window to check things out. The operator picked up and asked what my emergency was.

"There's a large pile of something burning on my front porch."

The operator alerted the fire department. I ran to my kitchen, Godfrey in step behind me. I snatched my small fire extinguisher from the counter near the stove, and went out the back door. I could already hear the fire trucks as I ran around to the front. The fire was eating my wood door. I sprayed the base. The flames grew larger. I stepped away from the heat and retreated to my lawn. Godfrey sat next to me. We stared at the house. Two fire trucks and one police cruiser barreled up the street.

It took the fire department fifteen minutes to get the fire out. My door was gone. When I stepped inside, I noticed singe marks on my great Aunt Violet's grandfather clock. The entryway floor would have to be replaced. And, I saw painting in my future.

"Ms. Jackson."

I turned and saw two officers enter.

"Officer Jacobs." I nodded to the other officer. I didn't know him. Officer Jacobs was in my house a few months ago when Godfrey found a severed hand in my backyard.

Officer Jacobs took out his notebook and a pen.

"Just start at the beginning."

Thirty minutes later, Officer Jacobs and his partner, Officer Sims, left me to begin cleaning up the mess. The firefighters helped me close off the front door with heavy-duty plastic. One of them knew a handyman who could help me out. I called him. He arrived within an hour, measured the door, and left to get what he needed. Four hours and $500 bucks later, I was showered, and ready to get out of the house. My gym bag was already in my jeep. I needed to work off a little anger. Sages Den Martial Arts Academy in Benson fit the bill.

*****

"Dez? Murphy. Call me."

Not too wordy, that one. I erased the message and called him back. He answered on the first ring.

"I heard what happened. Are you all right?" Murphy asked.

"Yeah, I'm fine. There was a little damage. Insurance will cover it. How'd you hear about it?"

"I like to keep my ear to the ground." There was a short pause, then, "Have you found out anything useful, yet?"

"Actually, I have. I'm pretty confident we can rule out drugs or drug activity."

"I knew that. He was never into that kind of crap."

"Right, but I needed confirmation. People change." *Boy, do they.*

"So, what's next? Any idea who burned your door down?"

"No, I'm clueless about that one. The police can handle it. I've got plenty of other things to do. Speaking of which, I'm meeting up with a guy I know in North O. You feel like taggin' along?"

"Sure. I'm at the downtown library right now."

"I'll swing by to get ya. Give me 20 minutes. I'm leaving the gym now."

The line disconnected.

*****

Dennison Freight specialized in moving artifacts and other priceless artwork coast-to-coast, and worldwide. It opened in Omaha a few months ago. This was their third location in the United States. Now, I understood Clive Dixon's interest in the place. I drove the perimeter, passing the guarded entrance. A chain-link fence with barbed wire at the top, surrounded the grounds. I parked my Jeep on the east side, beneath burned-out street lights, to watch the docks. So far, I had counted 12 armed security guards in the back and two at the entrance. Paul's body was found further east, a few blocks from this side of the building.

After a few hours, I noticed two guards near the fence. I lowered my window and strained to hear. That proved futile, so I grabbed my camera and zoomed in for a closer look. One of the men jabbed his finger into the chest of the other. I snapped a few shots. The interaction escalated with the second man pushing the first one back. A short distance from them, another guard shouted something. The two men separated. One returned to the docks. The instigator walked the length of the fence, then disappeared around a corner.

I tossed my camera onto the passenger seat, started my Jeep and headed home. It was three o'clock in the morning. Godfrey, greeted me at the door with his mini football.

"Not now, Godfrey. It's late."

He wandered off, sulking. Oh, the guilt. I promised to take him to the park later. Now, though, I needed sleep.

*****

The next morning, Godfrey remembered. He jumped off the end of the bed, ran to the kitchen, and returned with his leash in his mouth. He dropped it on my face. I threw it to the floor. He picked it up and dropped it on me, again. Then, he barked and left the room.

Crap. I should have rescued a stupid dog.

I rolled out of bed and got cleaned up. From the top of the stairs, I heard a man's voice, and then a loud *thud* coming from the direction of the kitchen. I ran down the stairs, skipped the last few steps, and grabbed a bat from under the couch. I could hear Godfrey's low growl as I approached the kitchen with the bat raised.

"What the fuck are you doing here?" I asked.

Patrick Murphy lay sprawled out on the floor with Godfrey's mouth around his neck. He tried to move. Godfrey growled and adjusted his grasp. Murphy raised his left hand and waved at me to call off Godfrey. His other arm was trapped under 130 pounds of sheer muscle.

"It doesn't look like you're winning." I laughed, and set my bat down on the table. I walked around Murphy's legs to reach the fridge. "Orange juice?" I held up the container. Murphy's eyes pleaded with me. "No, I guess not. You seem indisposed at the moment." He tried moving his legs. Godfrey growled louder. I poured the juice and leaned back against the counter to watch.

I let a few seconds pass, then said, "Godfrey, release!"

Murphy sat up, coughing. I handed him the juice.

"I see you've met Godfrey." Godfrey sat next to Murphy and stared at the side of his head. "Get up slowly."

Murphy took a seat at the table.

"Nice dog," he said.

"I think so. He does his job well. What are you doing here? And, how the hell did you get in?" Murphy stared back at me. "Never mind, how. How about, why?"

He reached behind him for a bag on the floor near the door.

"I brought donuts." He smiled.

I sat across from him and waited.

"I wanted to touch base. See what you found out."

"I told you that I'd let you know when I had more information."

"You went to Dennison's last night."

"Yeah, I did. Apparently, so did you."

"Coincidence."

"What did you see?" I asked.

"I got the impression that they're movin' something they're not supposed to be movin'."

"What makes you think that?"

"I got inside."

My brow furrowed.

"Just listen. I got into building A. While I was in there, some of the guards opened a crate. It was filled with money."

"Counterfeit?"

"That's my guess."

"Why do you think Paul was around there the night he died?"

"I don't know. We lost touch about six months before he was murdered."

"What if he was working there, and discovered what was going down?"

"It's a possibility. Last time we spoke, he was looking for work."

"If I go asking around the place, that'll send up way too many red flags. We've gotta find another way to see if he was working there."

"How'd Dixon know my brother?

*****

By late afternoon, Haithem had gotten back to me on my background check for Paul. It turned out Paul got a job at Dennison's through a temp agency. He also knew Clive Dixon better than I originally thought. The two met in county lockup a year ago. That was a detail Clive left out when I spoke to him the first time. I hate having to talk to the same person about the same thing twice. He was officially on my shit list.

This time, I let Murphy tag along. I figured a little backup might come in handy. By 4 o'clock p.m., we were back in my Jeep searching for Clive. He wasn't in his usual haunts.

"There's one more place he might be." I turned on 24th and Lake Streets and drove south a few blocks. I pulled up outside Big Mike's Barber Shop, and let the Jeep idle at the curb. "I'll be right back."

Men filled all the chairs along the walls. Some played chess while they waited; others chatted about sports. Big Mike was trimming hair in the seat closest to the back. He nodded as I entered. Big Mike was an old friend of my dad's. They served together.

"Little Ms. D., come give me some sugar." I smiled, and walked back to give him a hug. "Been a while. When are you coming over for dinner? You know Marlene is going to give me all kinds of hell if she knows I saw you, and didn't tell you to bring your skinny butt to the house."

"Soon, I promise. Hey, Big Mike, have you seen Clive Dixon 'round today?"

"Matter of fact, that boy got himself picked up not 15 minutes ago."

"The police were here?"

"Sure was. Officer saw him outside the shop, cuffed him, and threw him into the backseat."

"Thanks." I turned to leave.

"Remember what I said! I don't want Marlene gettin' after me, ya hear?"

"I'll call her," I said, and opened the door to leave.

I got back into the Jeep and drove south.

"The police picked him up 15 minutes ago."

"Where are we going?"

"The police station."

"They're not going to just let you see him."

"He's got to post bail. I'll see what it is. If it's a few hundred, I'll get him out."

It took about 10 minutes to reach the downtown station. Murphy waited in the Jeep. Twenty minutes later, I was back in the Jeep.

"What happened?"

"He's not here."

"What do you mean, 'he's not here?' They just picked him up."

"I know. Something's not right." I pulled out of the lot and drove north toward Dennison Freight, and then east toward the area where Paul was found.

"Where are you going?"

"There are a bunch of old abandoned buildings east of Dennison Freight."

"What are you thinking?"

"I think someone got to Clive Dixon because he really did see something that night."

"What's Clive Dixon into?"

"Counterfeit paper, stolen art, that sort of thing."

"Shit."

"You think Paul and Dixon were working a deal?"

"It's a hunch, but it's all we have to go on."

I circled Dennison Freight, and went around to the east looking for a police car.

"Wait, slow up." Murphy pointed down an alley. A police car was parked and empty.

I drove around the next corner and stopped.

"I'll go up top and work my way down, and inside," Murphy said. "You try to get in through a window or door on the ground."

"We need to call OPD, Murphy."

"And say what? We don't know anything, yet."

I grabbed my gun and mini MagLite from the center console. "There's another light in the glove box." We got out of the Jeep. Murphy disappeared around the back of the building. I walked around to the front. The door was unsecured, but not open. I nudged it to create enough room for me to squeeze through. Inside, I waited, and listened before searching for Dixon. The floor was littered with broken needles. I passed rooms with mattresses. The place smelled like piss. A rat scurried past my foot. I thought about Murphy and smiled.

I heard voices in the distance, but couldn't make out what they were saying. I kept moving. As I got closer, I heard Clive Dixon.

"Man, I don't know what you're talking about. I didn't say nothin' 'bout you to Jackson. I swear."

I crouched behind several large steel drums, and peeked around to see what was going on. The officer had Dixon tied to a pole. He pointed his gun at him.

"I don't know anything, I'm tellin' you."

"Murphy was working with you," the officer said. "We know that. What'd you do with the money?"

A second officer came into view. He was ending a call on his cell phone.

"That was the boss."

The first officer looked at his partner. "And?"

"They found the money."

"Look, man, I won't tell nobody what I saw. I swear," Dixon said.

"We're done here." The officer's partner turned to leave. Gun drawn, a few steps away from the officer, Murphy appeared from behind a door.

"What happened to Paul Murphy?" Murphy asked.

"Whoa, put the gun down!" The officer guarding Dixon pointed his gun at Murphy. Murphy didn't move.

"I'm going to ask you one more time." His eyes stayed on the officer closest to him. "What happened to Paul Murphy?"

The second officer went for his gun. Murphy deflected the gun hand, grabbed him around the neck, and broke his arm. He dropped him to the ground. The other officer lined up to take out Murphy.

"Wait!" I stood up. The officer was in my line of sight.

In the distance, I heard my BFFs on their way. I'd called them before entering the building.

The officer lowered his gun. I eased up on mine. Then he raised it, and a single shot rang through the building. The sound echoed. His body lay on the ground at Clive Dixon's feet. The police arrived. We'd left Dixon and the officer's body where they were, so the police could see the scene the way we did. We'd propped the injured officer up against a wall, and kept our guns on him until the police found us. Internal affairs showed up. It turned out that they'd been watching these two officers for a while. Until now, they didn't have the evidence they needed to go after them. Now, they had Clive Dixon willing to tell everything he knew. He hadn't shut up since the officer shot himself.

Paul Murphy and Clive Dixon thought they could steal one of the crates filled with counterfeit money. The night they decided to do it, Officer Taylor and Officer Daley were working off duty at Dennison Freight. OPD suspected that the company was dealing in counterfeit money, and that the officers were helping to cover it up. When Taylor caught Paul Murphy outside with the crate, there was a struggle. Taylor broke Murphy's neck with a full Nelson and dumped his body. Daley helped cover up the murder. Neither of the officers knew what Dixon knew about that night, but were keeping an eye on him. When I started talking to Clive, they got nervous.

The police took our statements, assuring us that they'd follow up in the next day or so. That was more for Murphy's benefit; they didn't want him thinking he could go anywhere.

I dropped him at his motel across the river.

"You might want to think about getting a better place to stay."

"This is better than most places I've stayed during the last year."

"Yeah, but this one might have rats."

He smirked. "Thanks, Dez. I owe ya." He got out of the car. I watched him walk to the motel office. He still had a nice ass.

CHAPTER SIX

THE COLLECTOR

I'm not much of an art collector. Actually, I don't collect any art, unless weapons count. I've got lots of those, in various locations around my house. So, when a friend called asking for help finding an expensive piece of art she'd just purchased, I didn't think I was up for the task. Of course, my immediate thought was, "I hope it's not a diamond-studded whip." Been there, done that, got the t-shirt. Not goin' back.

I'd received Talia's panicked call two days ago.

"Dez, it's a painting by an up-and-coming artist. Everyone is buzzing about his work. I scored an invite to a gallery showing. This piece was the least expensive of the collection."

"What's it worth?"

"Somewhere in the neighborhood of $10,000 dollars."

"You're kidding me? How is that even possible?"

"He's very talented."

"Do I want to know what you paid for it?"

"Probably not."

"What happened to it?"

"I bought it last night. I planned to go home after the showing, but something came up at work. I didn't want to leave it in my car, so I put it in my office. It got late, and I was nervous about taking it back to my car, so I left it. This morning, it was gone."

"Any chance you told someone about this artist and how valuable the painting is?"

"Well," Talia got quiet.

She had a difficult time keeping her discoveries a secret. I'd known her in high school. She came from a wealthy family and never had to work for anything. She'd wear diamond earrings to school, order sushi delivered for lunch, and drove a new car -- a BMW -- that she crashed two months after her parents bought it. They replaced it with another new BMW. She was nice, but enjoyed being the center of attention. The only way she knew how to maintain the center, was to flaunt her purchases. During college, her parents' business went under, and they lost everything. She had to get a job for the first time. It was eye-opening for her, but she still didn't know how to stop being the center of attention. She didn't mean to brag. It was simply second-nature for her.

"Talia?"

"I was super excited about the gallery invite. I may have told a few people."

"Talia, you don't exactly work in the most upstanding of places."

She worked in a fitness gym in the marketing department. Not some elite or posh fitness studio. It'd only been in business six months. The marketing department consisted of Talia, and a guy named Bart, who helped out in exchange for a membership discount.

"I thought it'd be okay. I even hid it behind a file cabinet."

"Talia, there's not even a lock on your office door." I was sitting in my home office tossing a ball back and forth against the wall. "Did you file a police report?"

"Yes, but you know it's not a priority to them. I need your help."

Translation -- She's not going to pay me.

So, here I sat, in my Jeep two days later, mentally smacking myself upside the head, for agreeing to help her. Watching weight lifters go in and out of the gym was like waiting for water to boil. I was looking for two guys that Talia thought might have something to do with the missing painting. She said they seemed overly interested in her invitation to the gallery.

They usually came into the gym in the morning, and always together, but she hadn't seen them the morning that the painting disappeared.

I got out of my car and went into the gym.

Bart greeted me.

"Welcome to Cooper's."

"Is Talia around?"

"No, she didn't come in this morning."

That was a surprise.

"Maybe you can help me. I'd like information about membership."

"Oh, I can get that for you. Just wait one minute. I'll be back in a jiffy." Bart walked from behind the counter. He passed a table with papers strewn about, and stopped to straighten them. Then, he walked past a few pictures on the wall, and stopped to straighten those.

"Here you go."

I thanked Bart and returned to my Jeep to track down Talia. She answered, breathless, on the third ring.

"Where are you?" I asked.

"I had a hunch." She was whispering.

"What are you doing?"

"I found their addresses."

"Don't tell me what I think you're telling me. Seriously, Talia?"

"They haven't been to the studio. It turns out they live together. Not together, together. Just together."

"Where do they live?"

"It's a cute little house near Elmwood Park on Poppleton Street."

I wrote down the address. "What's up with your breathing?"

"Oh, I got out to check things out, then the phone rang. I didn't want to attract attention, so I ran back to my car."

"How about you leave the tracking to me?"

"Sure, sure. Of course, but I'm telling you, I saw some interesting things in their house."

"Go, Talia."

I disconnected the call and headed over to Poppleton Street.

*****

I arrived at the house on Poppleton Street as the two guys were leaving. One of them carried a cylinder that was about three feet long. They were dressed in business suits. I looked down the hill and saw Talia's Lexus. She ducked out of sight when she saw them.

Brilliant.

The guys were probably in their late twenties, and more like hummers than tanks. They pulled out of the driveway and drove west down the street and past Talia's Lexus. I followed, slowing briefly to point at Talia, who'd just popped her head back up, and motioned for her to leave. She shrugged, hands palm-up, trying to look innocent. I kept going.

A few minutes later, I caught Talia's Lexus in my rear view mirror. I shook my head. The guys were traveling west on Dodge Street. At 144th Street, they took the exit off of the West Dodge Expressway, and drove south. A few blocks past Pacific Street, they turned into a neighborhood, and stopped in front of a 70's style house. A man in his late 50s answered the door. I continued driving, turned around in a driveway, and parked on the opposite side of the street. Talia parked behind me and got out of her car to join me.

"What the hell are you doing?"

"What? I'm helping."

"How exactly are you helping?"

"This is the first time they've left all day. I bet that was my painting."

"Talia, I don't need your help, and if you were going to do this anyway, why'd you ask for my help?"

"Because you're a professional. And, you have cool gadgets."

I rolled my eyes and looked away.

"What do you think they're doing in there?"

"Talia, let's just wait and see what they do next."

"You're not going to check things out?"

I turned to face her. She was wearing a fitted yoga outfit. You know the kind. The pants suck to your body, then flare at the ankle, and the shirt accentuates your boobs.

"No, Talia. I'm going to watch and wait." I turned away, again.

She sort of huffed. Then, I heard the passenger door open. Before I knew it, Talia was running across the street, and up to a window on the side of the house.

You've got to be kidding, me. Why the hell do I help her?

I got out of my Jeep and met up with her.

"What do you plan to do, now?" I asked.

"I don't know. Maybe we'll see something. Or, hear something."

"Stay here."

I walked around to the front, climbed the steps, and rang the doorbell. The owner answered.

"May I help you?"

"Oh, thank goodness your home. My car," I pointed to Talia's Lexus, "Won't start. I'm not sure what the problem is. And, of course, I forgot to charge my cell phone. Darn battery is dead." I had it in my hand for effect, jiggling it about as though that might charge the battery. "Do you think I could use your phone?"

"Sure, come on in."

As I entered the foyer, I saw the two bodybuilders seated on a couch. The opened cylinder lay on a coffee table in front of them. I smiled. They smiled. It was all very cordial. The walls of the living room were adorned with several paintings. I fiddled with my phone, pretending to examine something on it, and managed to snap a few pictures. Something across the room caught my eye. It was Talia. She was waving to me from outside.

The owner returned with a cordless phone. I dialed Haithem Nazari's number. When he answered, and I rambled on about my car, he just laughed, and said, "Uh, huh." He knew the drill. I hung up.

"Thank you! I really appreciate your help."

"You're welcome. Is someone coming soon?"

"Yes, it shouldn't be too long." I turned to leave, then noticed a porcelain figurine on a table near the door. "Oh, this is lovely." I pointed to it. "And, your paintings -- I don't know much about art, but they're beautiful."

The man beamed.

"I'm a collector. In fact, I own a gallery in Benson." He pulled a card form his wallet, and handed it to me. "You should stop by."

"Oh, I will. Thank you." I read the card. "Mr. Richards."

"Cal." His dark brown eyes sparkled when he smiled. He was handsome in an understated way. "I didn't get your name."

"Elizabeth. Elizabeth Jackson."

"It's been a pleasure helping you, Ms. Jackson."

I left, fighting the urge to look over my shoulder. I walked to Talia's car. Thankfully, she left it unlocked. Of course, I shouldn't have been surprised by that. I slid into the driver's seat.

"What happened?"

I almost gave myself whiplash. She was laying across the backseat.

"Christ! Talia, you scared the shit out of me."

"Sorry. What'd you find out?"

"The owner of that house is an art collector and has a gallery in Benson."

"What about that cylinder they were carrying?"

"It was empty, but I don't know what, if anything, was inside it."

"Now what do we do?"

"We don't do anything. You go back to work. I'll check out the Benson gallery later."

"Here." She rummaged on the floor for something, then handed me the invitation to the show she attended. "You see that?" She pointed to an image. "That's my painting."

"I'll leave as soon as you pull away." I got out and returned to me Jeep.

*****

Splatter Art Gallery was located in the Benson neighborhood off of 62nd & Maple Streets. I'd looked up the website and learned that Mr. Richards was hosting an event at 7 o'clock tonight. Jeans and a T-shirt weren't going to cut it. Instead, I opted for black slacks, an emerald green silk blouse, and my knock-off Christian Louboutin Decollete 544 pumps. I let my curls hang down and added gold hoops to my ears.

The Benson business district was revitalized thanks to the success of a few new restaurants, bars, and a passionate community. One of the gyms I frequented, Sages Den Martial Arts Academy, was located just outside of the main business area. As I rolled up to 62nd & Maple Streets, people crowded the sidewalks eager to go into the nightclubs and restaurants. A small group gathered outside of Splatter, talking and smoking.

I found a parking spot on a side street, grabbed my clutch handbag, checking it for the essentials -- ID, throwing stars, lipstick, cash -- and placed my gun in my back holster. Five young guys past me as I walked to the crosswalk. One bumped into another when I smiled at him. They never learn.

Splatter wasn't much to look at from the outside. It was a squat, brick building with a bank of windows in the front, to the right of a single red door. A shingled overhang aged the entire building. I walked through the small group and entered a spacious gallery. About fifty people mingled in the space, chitchatting about the pieces. I maneuvered my way around and found Mr. Richards, near a bar, talking with a patron. He saw me as I approached and smiled.

"Ah, Ms. Jackson, so happy you could visit."

The woman next to him sipped her wine, waiting to be introduced.

"Victoria Reynolds, this is Elizabeth Jackson."

We exchanged a few meaningless pleasantries. He explained to her my enthusiasm for the art he collected, and that he felt it was his duty to teach me more about it.

"Elizabeth, let me show you around the gallery," Mr. Richards said. "Thank you for coming, Victoria. We'll talk, again, soon."

Victoria half-smiled and disappeared into the crowd.

"You look beautiful."

Heat rose in my cheeks. "Thank you."

"Let's begin on the right." He ushered me by my elbow, as he began to describe the first painting. After the third painting, I was bored. His phone rang. *Saved.*

"I do apologize. I need to take this call." He walked down a hall and entered another room. I decided to see what else the gallery had to offer, so I waited a minute, then followed.

I passed a few other guests, huddled in groups of two, and three, along the length of the hall. Every piece of wall space had something attached to it. Near the end of the hall a curtain draped from a door frame. A sign, affixed to the drape, read:

Employees Only. I glanced back at the people I'd passed. No one paid any attention to me. I slipped behind the curtain.

Opened and unopened boxes filled the entire area. Tables held paintings and frames. I wandered over to take a look at a few. The first one reminded me of a cat throwing up cat food. It was abstract, but that was the first image that came to mind. A picture on another table caught my eye. It seemed familiar. I went over for a closer look.

"See anything you like?"

Mr. Richards. Crap.

"These are very interesting." I pointed to a group of paintings on the table nearest to me, and flashed a smile.

"Yes, they are. These are part of our next exhibit."

"I see. And, this one," I pointed at the one that seemed familiar. "Who's the artist?"

"Oh, that's actually a reproduction. It's not part of the next exhibit. Victoria brought that by for me to see. How about we return to the main gallery? We don't like patrons seeing our -- mess."

He led me out of the back room.

*****

"Hey, Bart. Is Talia around?"

It was 9 o'clock a.m. I knew that if she wasn't in the gym, she would be soon. Besides her regular marketing duties, she handled the cardio kick class. It started at 9:30 a.m.

"She hasn't come in, yet. Are you joining up?"

I fiddled with the gallery invite she'd given me. "No, not today."

"That's a great piece." Bart pointed to the image of the painting Talia bought.

"I guess. If you like that sort of thing." I shoved it back into my bag. "Talia bought it."

"Really? Wow. Good choice."

"You're into art, huh?"

"Not really. I just know what I like when I see it, you know. Kind of like cars."

"Dez! You're in the studio bright and early." Talia walked in carrying a bedazzled pink gym bag. "Hi, Bart."

He smiled, and excused himself to answer the phone. I followed Talia to her office. She set her bag on top of the file cabinet.

"You saw it?" Talia asked, as I sat down in the chair across from her desk. I'd left her a message last night after I left Splatter.

"Not it, exactly."

"What do you mean?"

"Richards said it was a reproduction."

"A reproduction of a piece of art that was just released? Really? That's ridiculous."

"I know."

"What are you thinking?"

"I'm thinking I need to do some more checking on the two Hummers. Give me their registration information."

After I left the gym, I called my former colleague, Haithem, and asked if he'd run a background check on them. He agreed to do it in exchange for another date. Normally, I wouldn't fall prey to this sort of bribery, but Haithem had a rock-hard body, olive-colored skin, dark brown eyes, and dimples. I love dimples. Oh, and accents. The side benefit to accepting his bribe, was that he was paying.

Since I'd be waiting a while for Haithem to get back to me, I decided to follow-up with the OPD about my door. Last month, someone left me a gift on my front stoop. It burned down my door, singed my great aunt Violet's clock, ruined my entryway floor, and I had to paint the walls. I hate painting.

"Is officer Jacobs available?"

Officer Jacobs picked up the line.

"Ms. Jackson, I'm afraid we still don't have any information for you."

"Nothing at all?"

"Well, we thought we had a lead, but it turned out to be a dead end."

"What was it?"

"A guy named Alec Covington ring a bell?"

"No, should it?"

"We found a print at the scene. We ran it and his name came up."

"Who is he?"

"He's dead."

Officer Jacobs assured me that they were continuing their investigation. I couldn't shake the feeling that I should know this Covington guy, but I couldn't figure out why. The Star Wars theme song blared, and I answered my phone. Haithem had information about the two Hummers. They were dealing in forgeries. The only other person I knew who did that was Clive Dixon.

I headed toward 16th & Locust Streets. Clive was hanging outside his building smoking a cigarette. I pulled alongside the curb and lowered the passenger side window.

"What's up Ms. Dez?"

"Hey, I came across this." I showed him the image on the invitation.

"So?"

"What I mean is, this painting was purchased in a gallery a few nights ago. Then, it was stolen. Last night, I saw a reproduction of it."

"I ain't seen this one before."

"Any thoughts on who might do this type of work?"

Dixon stared at me for a beat, then said, "I can't be tellin' you those details. I got a reputation. You know I move this shit."

"My friend bought the painting. I'm just trying to find the original."

"Shit, these days, ain't no artist worth their nads needs the original to create the fake."

I thanked Clive, and headed for Splatter.

*****

Splatter was closed, but I saw Richards outside talking to Victoria Reynolds. They walked to a nearby cafe. I parked across from the restaurant. A short time later, the two Hummers arrived carrying a cylinder. They certainly were busy. I watched for about an hour, then the Hummers left. I had a choice to make -- follow them, or approach Richards. I opted for following the Hummers. I had a feeling Richards distanced himself from the people who created the forgeries.

The Hummers headed east toward downtown. They parked across from a tan brick building with a red-shingled overhang. I never realized how popular that ugly overhang thing was until now. They entered the building through a garage on 16th & Burt Streets. The building had a series of frosted windows that obstructed my view. I found a spot, a block south, between cars on 16th Street, got out, and walked north toward the building. This area of Omaha was maybe a mile north of downtown. The buildings are old, and a lot of them are empty. The owners are just waiting for the right development deal.

I walked around the building. Nothing. There were three ways in, and no way to see what was happening on the inside. I could either go back to my car, and wait, or knock on the door. If I knocked on the door, the guys might recognize me from the other day. That could be bad. I headed back to my Jeep. I rounded the corner at 16th & Burt Streets and bumped into Clive Dixon.

"Shit, what are you doing here?" he asked, as he straightened himself up.

"Same as you, apparently."

"Nah, I doubt that."

"What is this place?"

"What place?"

I gave him my best Cocker Spaniel look and folded my arms across my chest.

"Oh, you mean this place." He gestured to the building. "I don't know much about this place. I was headed somewhere else."

"Clive."

"Dez, you can't be coming 'round here messing up my business."

"I didn't know you had business over here, but seeing as you do, maybe you can help me out?"

He stared back at me, then shook his head, and said, "Nope."

"I told you before, I'm just looking for my friends painting. Whatever else is happening, whatever you're doing, I don't care."

He looked around and stuffed his hands in his jean pockets.

"Look, you're obviously going in there. All I need to know is if the painting is inside."

"Why can't you do it yourself?"

"There are two guys in there who might recognize me."

"If I do this for you, then you need to do somethin' for me."

I knew what was coming next.

"You have ta let that shit that happened a few months back, go. You can't be tellin' the police nothin' 'bout me."

"Fine."

"Good."

I walked back to my Jeep and waited.

Thirty minutes later, Clive strolled up to the passenger side of my Jeep. I rolled down the window.

"Well?" I asked.

"I didn't see nothin' like that painting you showed me." He was carrying a cylinder strapped across his back.

"What's that?"

"What?"

I pointed to the cylinder.

"A gift for Auntie Katrina."

I thanked Clive and returned to Cooper's Gym.

*****

I walked past Bart's car on the way into the gym. It was a Honda Civic Hatchback circa 2001. Talia had pointed it out to me before. I don't remember why, other than it was one of her ways of identifying whether or not a guy had any money. There were partially-opened boxes stacked in the back, papers and clothes littered the backseat, and the front passenger seat had a pile of body building magazines on it. Discarded energy bar wrappers and drink cans lay on the floor.

I entered Cooper's. Bart wasn't at the counter. I looked through the glass wall. He was giving a tour, and waved me through. I found Talia in her office.

"We can forget about the Hummers. They didn't steal it."

"How do you know?"

"That's kind of my thing, Talia. I investigate and rule things out."

"Okay, so what now?"

"Can you think of anyone else who might have taken an interest in your invitation to the show?"

She leaned back in her chair, thinking. "No, not really."

"Well, at least, you can file an insurance claim."

"You're quitting?"

"First of all, you're not paying me, so quitting doesn't apply to this situation. And, second, I've got other cases to investigate. I've done all I can here. You need to leave it to the police."

She started doing that annoying thing she always did when she wasn't getting her way. Her bottom lip jutted out, her eyebrows sulked, and she leaned forward, and rested her chin in her left hand. Then, she sighed, and waited. She could sit like this for hours. Okay, maybe not hours, but it sure as hell felt that way.

"Talia, just wait for the police to find it." I stood up, and walked to the door. Something caught my eye. I bent down and reached behind her file cabinet. "Your cleaning crew could do a better job." I tossed the energy bar wrapper into the garbage next to her desk, and left.

Bart wasn't in the main area of the gym when I left. I walked out to my Jeep and saw him getting into his Honda. I waved. He waved. Then, it hit me. I got into my car and followed Bart. He lived in an apartment complex north of 90th & Dodge Streets. I waited for him to go inside, and then I pressed buttons until someone answered. There's always someone willing to just buzz you in. I said I had a delivery, and that was all it took. His first initial and last name were listed on the mailboxes. It also happened to be the only name beginning with the letter b. Luck was on my side. His apartment was on the third floor.

It was lunch time, so he probably came home to eat. I figured I'd wait until he left, and then go in. Thirty minutes later, I picked the lock, and slipped inside.

There was barely enough room to walk from the front door to any other part of his apartment. There were boxes stacked atop boxes, crates overflowing with magazines -- I checked a few dates. They went back twenty years. There were piles of papers everywhere. An entire area was devoted to "As Seen on TV" health-related gadgets, supplements, and equipment. I snaked my way past a teetering group of file boxes to the back part of his apartment. There was a bathroom and two bedrooms. Door number one was his bedroom. It looked just like the living room. I tried door number two. It wouldn't open. Something blocked it. I shoved hard. It finally gave way.

The room was filled to the ceiling with sculptures, framed art, and more crates. I started searching for the painting. The art in the room was easily worth several thousand dollars.

Why would he keep it like this? I found Talia's painting, rolled up, on top of a crate near the window. The closet door was open. The frame leaned against the wall with at least ten others behind it. I grabbed the frame and the painting, then headed for the front door.

I heard keys jingling outside the door. There wasn't anywhere for me to hide. Bart entered the room.

"What are you doing here?" His face flushed. His eyes darted from one pile to the next, then back to me.

"Look, Bart. I don't give a shit about all this other stuff, but I'm taking this with me."

"No, you can't. I need it."

"Um, Bart. You stole it. That's a crime."

"So is breaking into someone's apartment."

"True, but I'm guessing that you don't want anyone seeing -- this." I gestured toward the various piles of stuff. "I'll return this to Talia, and if you agree to leave her alone, then I'll encourage her not to press charges."

"But, she already reported it to the police." The air escaped his chest and he fell back against the door, his hands covering his face.

"You obviously have a problem. I'm sure something can be worked out."

His eyes met mine. They filled with tears. "I know I need help."

I left Bart, and returned to Cooper's gym. Talia was thrilled to get her painting back, but took a little convincing about not pressing charges against Bart. My good deed done for the week, I returned home. Godfrey waited for me in the bay window as I pulled up. I walked up the stone steps, happy to see my new steel door. I forgot to check for mail. I walked back down the steps, and across the lawn. Then, my mailbox exploded.

CHAPTER SEVEN

THREE'S COMPANY

My day was definitely off to a bad start. I was scheduled to meet a new client in fifteen minutes and one of my tires was flat. I left a message on her voice mail, and spent the next twenty minutes struggling with the damn tire. Finally on my way, I rolled into the parking lot of Zio's Pizzeria off of Dodge Street, located a parking spot, and headed inside. A brunette, looking a bit out of place, sat in a booth farthest to the left of the doors, near the windows. I approached the table.

"I'm Dezeray Jackson. You wouldn't happen to be Meg Tyler?"

She fidgeted with an extra straw. "Yes, yes I am. Thank you for meeting me."

"Thanks for agreeing to meet me here."

"I've never been here before."

"Yeah, I kinda got that impression." I tossed my leather jacket into the corner of the seat along with my satchel, then sat across from her. She was probably about 5'6" tall, and thin. Too thin, really. "How can I help you?"

She took a long drink from her glass before answering. "I want to know if my husband is cheating on me." She set the glass back onto the table, and picked up the straw, again.

Here we go.

"What makes you believe that he is?"

"A hunch."

"Do you have any actual proof? Are there any tell-tale signs? Lipstick on a collar? Anything?"

She stared at her hands. The tremor was barely noticeable. She set the straw down. "No." She set a large manila envelope onto the table, and slid it across to me. I opened it. My eyes met hers. A smile formed at the corners of her mouth.

"Everything you need is in there. I included an initial payment of three thousand dollars. There's a picture, his work address, our address, his usual schedule, and a list of places he likes to -- frequent."

"And, what do you plan to do if I find out that he is cheating?"

"I -- I don't know, yet."

"Why come to me?"

"I've heard that you're discreet. Obviously, my husband is a powerful man. You recognized him, don't you?"

"Yes. So, this about the money, then?"

"No, not really."

Yeah, right. I thanked Mrs. Tyler, assuring her that I'd be in touch, and grabbed a slice to go.

*****

First up, his gym. He worked out at New Reality Fitness. It was an upscale, state-of-the-art facility that catered to the rich and famous in Omaha, NE. I happened to have a membership. It was a gift from a client. He considered it a retainer.

"Hi, Malcolm." I greeted the twenty-something personal trainer at the desk. "Filling in?"

"Hi, Ms. Jackson. Yeah, for a bit." He swiped my card.

"You wouldn't happen to know if Josh Tyler is here this morning, would you?"

"As a matter of fact, he just arrived. I think he was headed for the racket ball courts."

"Great, thanks. Could I get a racket?"

"Ms. Jackson, we're still looking for a self-defense instructor if you're interested." He said, as he handed me the racket.

"I'll give it some thought."

I stopped in the locker room. I always keep workout gear in my Jeep. You never know when you're going to have time to get a workout in. Best to be prepared. I grabbed my digital button camera and attached it to my shirt, then headed to the courts in the basement.

The basement was brightly lit, much like the rest of the facility. There were ten courts. A window in the door allowed for some viewing, other than that, there was no observation area. I walked down the hall, stopping at each door, to peak into the rooms. I found Tyler in the last one. He didn't have a partner. I knocked, then entered, deflecting the ball as it flew at me.

"Nicely, done." Tyler grinned and caught the ball.

"You up for a game? There doesn't appear to be anyone else playing this afternoon."

"Yeah, that would be great. I hate practicing alone. What's the fun in that?"

"I don't play all that often."

"I'll take it easy on you. Promise."

Josh Tyler was an investment banker. He was about 6' tall, in his mid-to-late 40s, had wavy brown hair, and a fit body. He schooled me for about an hour, stopping a few times to correct my lack of technique.

"Anytime you want a few more lessons, let me know. I'm here every day around this time." He toweled off, and drank water from a squeeze bottle. I wiped the sweat from my face. I'd forgotten my water bottle.

"Great game. I'm going to head up to the snack bar. I'm famished!"

"I'll join you. You really heated up my appetite."

"Okay, I'll see you up there. I'm just going to stop in the locker room real quick." I smiled.

I showered and did a quick change before meeting Tyler. Sitting around in stinky, sweaty clothes isn't my idea of a good time. He was seated at a table with a view of the indoor pool. I walked over.

"I grabbed a few sandwiches and a water for you. Hope you don't mind."

"No, not at all. Thank you." *He's smooth this one. Or, more likely, controlling.* I took the seat opposite his.

"It's turkey & cheese. Most people like that."

"You're right, I certainly do." A bag of chips would have been a nice touch. Of course, this being a fitness place, they didn't have the good ones.

"So, Dezeray Jackson, what do you do when you're not playing racket ball?"

"I'm a financial planner. Independent." I took a bite of my sandwich.

"Ah. I'm an investment banker. Maybe you've heard of Wilson-Tyler Financial?"

"Josh Tyler! It's been too long." A woman with long, blonde hair approached our table. Tyler stood and kissed her on the cheek. "Sylvia, it has been a long time."

He introduced us. Sylvia held onto his hand a little longer than I'd expect from a long lost acquaintance. And, her forced smile upon seeing me revealed a hint of, what was it, exactly - jealousy? Yep. He was cheating. She joined us, and we engaged in idle chitchat while he and I finished our food.

"It was a pleasure meeting you, both. Thanks, again, for the sandwich, Josh."

That elicited a raised eyebrow from Sylvia. I smiled, grabbed my gym bag, and headed for the exit.

*****

Famed investment banker, Josh Tyler was hospitalized last night.

I heard the news as I walked back into the kitchen to grab an apple.

His doctors aren't releasing too many details except to say that Mr. Tyler's condition is stable and he's resting. Police officers were called to the hospital. We will update you as more information becomes available.

That's not good. A commercial for Lucky Charms came on. The phone in my office cut through the TV noise. I caught it on the last ring.

"Ms. Jackson, my name is Kiley Winslow. I'm Josh Tyler's assistant. Do you know who he is?"

"How may I help you?"

"I'm sure you heard about the incident. Mr. Tyler would like you to come to the hospital."

She gave me the hospital location, and his room number.

"You should have no problem getting in to see him." Her voice wavered a bit.

I thanked her and hung up the phone. Why would Josh Tyler contact me? Godfrey, my Rottie, stood in the doorway of my office staring at me. When I didn't acknowledge him, he barked. I pushed past him. He followed me to the kitchen and hovered as I filled his dish. His food disappeared in three bites, and I let him outside. Ten minutes later, I was out the door, and on my way to Methodist Hospital on 83rd & Dodge Streets.

Josh Tyler's room was on the seventh floor. The last time I visited Methodist hospital was when my sister died seventeen years ago. I wasn't looking forward to reminiscing, and I hate hospitals. I can't shake the feeling that I'm going to walk in fine, and then leave with some sort of disease.

Hospitals always smell bad. They're okay until you get up onto the patient floors. Then pungent odors emerge from every room. I located Josh Tyler's room. A police officer was posted outside. I showed my ID, and he opened the door.

Tyler lay propped up in his bed tethered to an IV. The window shades had been opened, flooding the room with sunlight. The room was hot.

"Financial planner, huh?" He struggled to smile. "I asked my assistant to find the best private detective in Omaha. It turns out they're pretty busy, but you came recommended."

Ouch.

"I'm guessing you showing up at the club yesterday wasn't a coincidence."

"No, but I am a member." I set my bag on a chair and removed my jacket.

"My wife hired you?"

"Yes."

"She's paranoid."

"Why am I here?"

"I want you to find out who's trying to kill me."

"You already know I can't do that."

"The police are obviously questioning my wife. So, she won't be needing your services." He adjusted his body and winced. "And, I'll pay you better."

"Let's say that I decide to take your case. What can you tell me?"

"I have Hepatitis A. Do you know how that happens?"

I shook my head. I was pretty sure I didn't want to know.

"It happens when people eat shit."

My ears perked up at that. What kind of person does that?

"The doctors think that someone has been putting it into my food."

Wow. Someone really hates this guy. The short list was his wife, and whoever his mistress is -- Sylvia, maybe?

"The doctors say I'll recover. It's going to take some time, but someone wants me either dead, or in a lot of pain."

I pulled a notebook from my bag. Paper and pen was still better than all the technology out there. I flipped it open, wrote today's date at the top, and his name. "So, who do you think did it?"

"Besides my wife? I'm not sure."

"Have you been having an affair?"

He smoothed the blanket that covered him from the waist down. His left hand scratched his ear. Then, he said, "No."

"Who is Sylvia to you?"

He swallowed hard, and reached for a cup of water on the table next to his bed. "She's an old friend."

"Friend?"

"It was a long time ago."

"So, your wife has a reason not to trust you."

"It happened during our separation." He turned his head to look outside.

"When did it get rekindled?"

His head snapped back in my direction.

"I'm a detective, remember?"

*****

Tyler mentioned that his assistant had Sylvia's contact information. I headed to Wilson-Tyler Financial on 168th & Center Streets. It was a two-story brick building near several restaurants. My stomach rumbled when I passed Roja. I made a mental note to stop there for lunch.

A centrally-located reception desk, with the company's name on a wall behind it, confirmed that I was in the right place. A young woman sat in a raised, leather chair, at the semi-circular desk, answering calls. She smiled as I approached. She raised her index finger and mouthed that she'd be just a minute.

"Thank you for waiting. How may I help you?"

"I'm here to speak with Mr. Tyler's assistant, Kiley Winslow."

The receptionist directed me to a hallway to the left of the reception area.

"Mr. Tyler's office is at the end. Just go right in."

This firm was one of the top investment companies in Omaha. All of my money was with an internet-based bank. I never thought to move it after I relocated to Nebraska. I'd have to remember to pick up one of Wilson-Tyler's brochures on my way out.

The door opened as I arrived at the end of the hall.

"Ms. Jackson? Come in. I'm Kiley."

She ushered me into a sitting area to the right of her desk. A dark wood door was to the left and flanked by windows. The blinds were closed.

"Please, make yourself comfortable. Let me just get Mrs. Thorpe's contact information." She walked behind her desk and grabbed a small envelope. "Here you go." She sat on a couch across from me.

"Ms. Winslow, have you ever met Mrs. Thorpe?"

Kiley Winslow's face flushed, and then she said, "No, well, I mean, not really."

I waited. There was more.

"She came to the office a few months ago -- once."

"I understand that Mr. Tyler and his wife were separated at some point."

She fidgeted with a pen in her hand.

"Do you happen to know when that was?"

"It was six months ago."

"How long were they separated?"

"Five months."

"When did they get back together?"

"Last month."

"How long have you worked for Mr. Tyler?"

"Two years."

"I bet you know everything about him."

Her face flushed, again.

"I know that he was seeing Mrs. Thorpe while he and his wife were separated, and that he stopped seeing her when he reconnected with his wife," I said.

Kiley's eyebrow scrunched forming little wrinkles between her eyes.

"I suspect that his relationship with Mrs. Thorpe didn't end right away, or perhaps ever."

She smoothed her skirt. "I don't really know the details."

I smiled and nodded. "Hmm. Okay, then. When did you start seeing Mr. Tyler?"

"I - I don't know what you're talking about." She stood. I stood. "If you don't mind, Ms. Jackson, I have work to do."

"Well, thank you for this information." I held up the envelope, turned, and left the office.

*****

"Have you ever been cheated on, Ms. Jackson?"

I'd decided to pay Mrs. Tyler a visit. The police were gone, and I thought she might be willing to open up to me.

"No." We were in her kitchen. I could fit two of my kitchens in this one spot.

"You're lucky."

More like, not stupid.

"We were happy - once." She was cleaning a BlendTec blending jar. "Before the money."

"Do you have children?" I hadn't noticed any pictures as we walked to the kitchen. In fact, there weren't even any pictures of them.

"No, not yet. We tried, but it's been difficult. Josh travels a lot."

"How did you find out about Sylvia Thorpe?"

She picked up the BlendTec and pushed it farther back on a counter, then turned to look at me.

"Josh's assistant."

"What did Ms. Winslow say?"

"The first time, she didn't say anything specifically. I'd called to talk with Josh. I had a little cold, and my voice was raspy. She thought I was Mrs. Thorpe."

"Why was that a flag to you?"

"I'm not sure. It might have been the way Kiley stammered when she realized her mistake."

"Is she the one who told you Josh was seeing Mrs. Thorpe during your separation?"

"Yes, and Josh didn't deny it when I confronted him."

"But, you got back together knowing that the relationship might not be over."

"Josh assured me that it was, but," she wiped the counter with a cloth. "Kiley mentioned that Mrs. Thorpe had phoned the office several times, and Josh left to meet her."

"Are you close to Kiley? Why would she tell you?"

"We're friendly, I guess." She tossed the towel in a bin under the sink. "I always made sure to send her a gift on her birthday, holidays, and Secretary's Day. Maybe she felt obligated."

I noticed a small shot glass near the sink. There was a pale liquid in it. Meg Tyler followed my eyes.

"Oh, I forgot that one." She turned the faucet on, cleaned out the glass, and placed it into a Bosch dishwasher.

"I hear those are super quiet."

"Oh, yeah, they're great." Her voice trailed off. "Expensive. It was Josh's idea. Everything top of the line."

"Here." I slid the envelope containing her initial payment across the island counter top. "Everything is in there, including your deposit."

"But, I don't understand."

"You have your answer. And, I really didn't have much to do with that."

"Yes, I suppose I do."

"Did the police tell you that your husband was poisoned?"

"Yes, and I can't believe it. They questioned me, of course, but I told them about Mrs. Thorpe. They didn't know about her." She pushed her hair back behind her ears. "I still love my husband."

*****

Sylvia Thorpe's personal assistant led me through a large foyer and a stylishly-appointed, sparkling white living room. I followed her through French double doors, onto a terrace overlooking a golf course. Mrs. Thorpe was seated at a table, sipping white wine. It was 5 o'clock somewhere.

"Can I get you anything?" the assistant asked.

"No, thank you."

"Ms. Jackson, is it?"

I nodded.

"The woman from the club?"

I nodded, again.

She invited me to sit down. I pulled out the chair. It scraped across the terrace floor. She winced at the sound.

"I understand that you were seeing Mr. Tyler."

"Yes, it was months ago, darling." Her finger circled the rim of her wine glass.

Darling?

"When did you start seeing him, again?"

She set down her glass. "What makes you think I have?"

"A hunch."

"Ms. Jackson, what exactly is this about?"

"Mr. Tyler believes someone is trying to kill him."

She scoffed. "Who, on earth, would want to kill that man?"

"A jealous lover, maybe?"

A poodle came to the table. She reached down to pick it up, and placed it on her lap. She stroked its fur.

"If you're looking for a jealous lover, then perhaps you should be speaking with his assistant, Ms. Winslow."

"Why's that?"

"Oh, come now. You're a detective. I'm sure you can figure it out."

There are a few things that piss me off. Deep dish pizza when I was expecting New York style. Over-bearing men. Puntable, yappy dogs, and condescending wealthy bitches who've never had a job.

"True, I certainly can, and already did, but this is more about you."

"I have nothing to hide."

"Are you still seeing Mr. Tyler?"

"Oh, once in a while -- when I get an itch." She took another sip of her wine.

"When was the last time you got scratched?"

"Touché." She set the dog down. "I saw Josh three nights ago."

"Do you think his wife knows?"

"I'm sure she does." She rested her back against the chair and played with a large sapphire and diamond ring on her left hand. "How could she not? What woman doesn't know, in her heart of hearts, that her husband is playing in someone else's pond?"

"You're married?"

"Thirty wonderful years."

"Does your husband know about Josh Tyler?"

"My husband is too busy banging his partner's wife to care what I do."

I thanked Mrs. Thorpe for her time.

Back in my Jeep, I finished a Coke I'd picked up on my way over. I scanned the neighborhood. All the money in the world, and all they do is buy more crap, sleep around, and drink. Idiots. This was my third time, in a month, to this same neighborhood because of a cheating spouse case. This is why I have no plans to get married.

My phone rang. The caller ID said it was Mr. Tyler. I let it go to voice mail.

*****

"Let me see if I understand what you've been up to. Stop me, if I leave anything out."

I sat in a chair in Josh Tyler's hospital room.

"You didn't think to mention to the police that you're having an affair with Sylvia Thorpe. Your wife still loves you even though she knows about Sylvia, but not about Kiley."

That got his attention. His smug expression changed to concern.

"Yeah, I figured that out pretty quickly. What I don't know, yet, is who poisoned you. It could be any one of them, or even Thorpe's husband."

A young, curvy nurse entered the room. Her blonde hair fell forward as she leaned to adjust his pillow and check his vitals. He smiled at her. She left the room.

"Give it a rest, would you? If you're little head did a little less of the thinking, you wouldn't be here."

"What are you talking about?"

I rolled my eyes and sighed. How can a person be financially successful, and be such a complete tool?

"Let's think about this logically. You were poisoned through food. Whoever did it, started putting crap into your food at least a few weeks ago. They would have had to do it repeatedly. And, they would have had to either be infected or know someone who was."

"Kiley was sick a few weeks ago. She said something about the stomach flu."

"That's a start, but you're going to have to tell the police everything you know."

"I hired you so I could avoid all of that."

"The police are going to keep investigating. Eventually, they'll find out about Sylvia and Kiley. It won't take them long, either. What were you planning to do once I found out who poisoned you?"

His expression was blank.

"You hadn't thought that far."

"Just find out which one of them did it, and then I'll decide how to handle the police. What if it was Meg? I don't want anything to happen to her."

Maybe he should have thought about that, before he dipped his stick in another woman's pool. I left the hospital. It was time to hack a few email accounts. I called Haithem Nazari.

A few hours later, I had email exchanges between Kiley, Meg, and Sylvia. The ladies all knew about the other, but discovered it over the course of the last two months. Judging by their exchanges, things were heating up, but they weren't pissed at each other. That was refreshing. There was a lot of discussion about making him feel the pain they felt. What didn't make sense was the finger pointing. Why would Kiley out Sylvia, and Sylvia accuse Kiley? Did something else happen between them? Or, was Kiley, in her own way, simply more loyal to Meg. And, why did Meg hire me? I knew the emails weren't enough to prove one of them poisoned Josh Tyler. Still, it was a start.

I returned to Josh Tyler's office to talk with Kiley. Of the three women, she was the most likely to spill the details. She was sitting at her desk when I entered. She looked up.

"Ms. Jackson? Was the information I provided incorrect?"

"No, it was fine. I just have a few more questions."

She set down her pen, stood up, and walked to the sitting area. "Can I get you something to drink?"

Not a chance. "I'm good, thanks." I sat across from her. "Is that what you do for Mr. Tyler?"

"What do you mean?"

"Get his drinks for him." She nodded *yes*. "What does he usually drink?"

"Coffee, black, two sugars."

"Every morning?"

"Uh, huh. Why?"

"The doctors say he was poisoned, but I think you already knew that."

"Poisoned? But, how? I would never."

I held up my hand to stop her. "Please. I've seen the emails."

Her shoulders sagged. It was like watching the air escape from a balloon.

"It wasn't my idea."

"When did you all find out about each other?"

"Sylvia told Meg about me a few months ago."

"Whose idea was it to poison Mr. Tyler?"

She started ringing her hands, then smoothed her skirt, and stood up. She walked to a nearby window.

"We weren't trying to. I mean, there was this report on the news. Meg mentioned it. We'd all seen it."

"What report?"

"A nurse in Arizona was accused of injecting fecal matter into her husband's IV." She turned to look at me. "We weren't going to do that. We just wanted to make him sick."

"You all did it."

"Yeah."

"How?"

"Meg was putting it into his morning smoothie. Sylvia put it into his drinks whenever they were together. And,"

"You put it into his coffee."

She nodded *yes.*

"Why did Meg hire me?"

"She wasn't feeling right about our plan. She wanted proof."

*****

There's an old saying about a woman scorned, and hell, or something. Josh Tyler's lucky all that happened was a severe stomach ache. I reported what I learned about Meg, Sylvia, and Kiley to the police. Josh Tyler wasn't going to do it, but attempted murder isn't something I could ignore. It's too bad the women took matters into their own hands. Meg could've divorced the asshole, and taken half his money. I felt sorry for Kiley. She'd get the brunt of the punishment, because she didn't have the money to hire a high-priced lawyer. And, Sylvia Thorpe would never see the inside of a prison cell. Life truly isn't fair. That bitch deserved to have her ass handed to her.

CHAPTER EIGHT

BUYER BEWARE

My phone jolted me from a great dream about a sexy cowboy with amazing abs. He was tall. His opened shirt exposed lean muscle and a dark, tanned body. He tilted his hat to greet me. We exchanged a few pleasantries as we leaned against a wood fence. He offered to teach me to ride. His outstretched hand invited me to join him. I hesitated, and then *poof!* He disappeared. Damn phone.

I felt around on the bedside table for my phone. "Hello?" I could barely make out the time on the clock. It was 2 a.m. "This better be good, dammit."

"I need to speak to you. Now. Meet me at Eddy's."

"Who the fuck is this?"

"Katrina."

Ah, shit. I hung up. Godfrey, my Rottie, kicked my feet. I propped myself up. He was dream running. I dragged my body out of bed, grabbed my clothes off a nearby chair, and shuffled to the bathroom. Teeth brushed, hair contained in a ponytail and baseball cap, I headed out the door and to my Jeep.

I took my time getting to Eddy's, stopping through a 24-hour drive through along the way. I needed coffee and fries. And, maybe a pastry. Yeah, I definitely needed a pastry.

Eddy's was closing up for the night. The bouncer waved me past the people milling about outside, and told me where to find Katrina. She was in Eddy's back office, pacing. I was surprised to find her alone.

"Where's your guard?"

"Never mind that. I need you to do something for me." She stopped pacing long enough to light a cigarette, ignoring the "no smoking" sign on Eddy's desk.

"I thought you quit."

"So did I." She took a long drag, exhaled and said, "Shut the door."

I sat in a chair opposite the desk. "What's so important you had to wake me up at 2 o'clock in the morning?"

She sat across from me. Smoke billowed around her. She put the cigarette out on an empty plate.

"I want you to find someone for me."

"Who?"

"That's part of my problem. I don't know who exactly."

"What do you know?"

"I was working a connection."

Translation -- she was making a deal.

"What happened?"

"What do you know about Bitcoins?"

I shrugged, and said, "A little."

"Well, I've been watching that market for a while. It's quick and it's clean."

Translation -- untraceable.

"And?"

"I wanted to test the waters."

"What happened?"

"He didn't come through."

"How much are you out?"

"About 20 thousand dollars."

"Do you know anything about the seller?"

"Nothing worthwhile. It's the darknet. You're not supposed to know much."

"When did the transaction take place?"

"It was supposed to happen today."

"How do you know it's just not late?"

"It wasn't at the agreed upon drop site."

I hate drug cases. It's never easy, and it's always messy.

"If I find your connection, then what?"

"I'll take care of it from there. Don't worry."

Right. Katrina's way of taking care of things wasn't anything I wanted to be a part of.

"I'm out." I stood to leave.

"You owe me, remember."

"And, you know there are certain lines I don't cross."

"You won't have to. All I want is a name. You don't even have to give me a location." She lit another cigarette.

"I'll think about it."

"Dez, I don't have time for this shit. Find him."

"How do you know it's a *him*?"

"I don't. I'm playin' the odds."

I took a deep breath and met her eyes. "I do this, and we're done."

"Agreed." Her long blonde hair fell in front of her shoulders. She pushed it back. "For now."

*****

Haithem Nazari is my go-to guy for all things technical. The man is brilliant. I don't understand most of what he's talking about when he geeks out, but as long as he gets me the information I need, I don't care. I had called him, after leaving Katrina, to ask about black market trading. I was surprised when I answered.

"Tor."

"Who?" I asked.

"You either need Tor or Free Market, then you can search from there. Your client is probably using Tor. It's more popular."

"So walk me through Tor."

"Tor is a browser. Inside Tor, there are services. Essentially, Tor allows users to access the internet with a high degree of anonymity. Tor services gives users anonymous access to various websites. That's where you can get into any black market deal, but there are legitimate reasons to use Tor and Tor services."

"Are you saying that there's no way to track down the person behind the transaction?"

"Well, I wouldn't say that. It's not impossible. It's more like, improbable. It can take a long time, even for skilled hackers."

"I don't have months to figure this out."

"Then you need the services of an exceptional hacker."

"And, where might I find one?"

"Tor." He laughed. "Just kidding. I've got a little time today. I'll see what I can find out."

I hung up the phone, leaving Haithem to his geekdom. For the moment, there wasn't much I could do to solve Katrina's problem, so I returned my focus to my own case. Over the years, I'd tried to find more information about my sister's murder. Every lead died. Then, when I came back home to Omaha, I started receiving gifts. Okay, some people wouldn't consider them gifts, but what can I say, I'm an optimist. The latest one was a note. All it said was North Downing. The first gift was my mailbox. It blew up. I know what you're thinking, but it wasn't meant to hurt me. Someone just wanted my attention. A note followed that one urging me to reconsider my relocation to Omaha. Now, I have a P.O. Box. The second gift was my new front door. Actually, it was the fire that ate my door, and that I replaced. The new door is steel. I didn't get a note after that one.

North Downing made no sense to me. This was the first I'd heard of it. None of the police records from my sister's file, which is officially classified as a cold case, made any reference to it. Was it a place? A person? I had no idea, but it was time to try to find out. I grabbed the case file from a cabinet in my office and began reading it. The last time I looked at any of the old information was more than ten years ago.

Incessant banging on the front door broke my concentration. Godfrey started barking and barreled down the stairs from my room. I looked through the peephole. It was one of Katrina's guards.

"What?" I asked after sidestepping Godfrey to open the door.

"Katrina wants to know what you found out."

I cocked my head like a Cocker Spaniel. It's my favorite, *I can't believe you asked me such a stupid question* look. "It's only been a few hours. Is she smokin' her own stuff these days?"

He handed me a small, folded piece of paper.

"What's this?"

He shrugged.

I read the note.

"I thought she didn't know anyone connected to her deal?"

He shrugged, again, and then turned to leave.

*****

Katrina's note led me to Clive Dixon. I wasn't clear how or why she thought he was involved, but at least it was somewhere to start.

Clive is a low-level art dealer. And, by dealer, I mean that he moves stolen art. Some of it's real, but most of it's not. He gave up dealing drugs. He's sort of risk-averse. Katrina let him walk away as a favor to his older brother. I don't know the entire story there. I'm pretty sure it's a good one, though.

Clive likes to hang out down on Locust street in North Omaha. He works out of an old, abandoned building that his brother owns.

The stench of backed up sewage filled my nose when I opened the door. I covered my mouth forcing the bile that crept up the back of my throat, into retreat. The heavy, steal door, slammed behind me. The main area was large. Exposed pipes lined the ceiling and brick walls. I heard dripping. There wasn't much furniture except a desk, two chairs, and an old, over-stuffed couch near the back.

Somewhere down a hall to my right, I heard footsteps. A short time later, Clive Dixon entered the room.

"What the fuck are you doing here?" He shouted.

"Why ya so jumpy, Clive?"

"I need to remember to lock the damn door." He walked over to the desk and tossed a paper he'd been holding, onto it. "You didn't answer my question."

"I'm looking for someone who's dealing in bitcoins. You know anybody like that?"

"Bitcoins?"

"Yeah, Bitcoins."

He made a show of scratching his head and thinking before taking the seat behind the desk. I took the opposite chair.

"What would I want with a bunch of volatile cyber shit?"

"So, then, you do know people."

"What we talkin' 'bout, exactly? Art or drugs?

"Drugs."

"Nah, nobody would be that stupid. Not at my level."

"What if it was someone trying to screw over another dealer. Someone local, for instance?"

He leaned back and thought about it, then said, "Are we talking about Katrina?"

I nodded.

He sat up. "Shit. She knows I don't deal anymore. What'd she say?"

"She's under the impression that you know someone that she'd be interested in having a chat with real soon."

"There's this one dude, but he's outa Lincoln."

I stared at him, waiting for him to continue.

"A few months back, I was moving merchandise to a new location in Lincoln. I came across this dude. Said he knew my brother from way back, and would I be interested in working with him. Since I know better than to shit where I eat, I said no thank you, and headed out."

"What was the deal?"

"I don't know no specifics, but he did mention somethin' 'bout internet black market. That's not how I roll, so I split."

"You remember his name?"

"All I know is he goes by Noble. Don't know if that's his last name, his street name, or what."

"Did you ask your brother about him?"

"Nah. Never came up."

I left Clive and headed to Lincoln. It was an hour drive west of Omaha. I gave Haithem a heads up that I'd be there after lunch.

*****

Haithem met me at Yai Yai's Pizza on "O" Street in downtown Lincoln. I spotted him at a table in the back. There was a light after-lunch crowd. I made my way through the narrow space, inhaling the intoxicating aroma of sauce, spice, mouth-watering add-ons, and beer. My stomach growled. I waved to Haithem and motioned that I planned to order a slice. Beer in hand, I settled into a seat across from him.

Haithem handed me a small paper with the name William Bell on it.

"Who's this?" I asked.

"I think that's your guy. I won't bore you with the details." He sipped his beer.

An employee shouted my name. My Mediterranean slice was ready. After retrieving my tin-style plate, and settling back into our table, I took a bite. My eyes closed, and I think I moaned. When I opened my eyes, Haithem was staring at me, smiling.

"Been that long, has it?"

"Something like that." I returned my slice to its plate. "So, who is William Bell?"

"Just your everyday, ordinary guy. He works as an accountant for a local firm." He reached over and grabbed the roll from my plate, spread butter on it, and took a bite. "You weren't going to eat this, right?"

I smiled. He knew I was there for the pizza. During college, I spent a lot of hours in this place. There used to be a pool hall next door. The combination of world-class beer, pizza, and suckers was irresistible to me.

"The question I have now is, 'how is William Bell connected with Noble.'"

"Who's Noble?"

"Low-level drug dealer. I suspect he was trying to make a move."

"Can't help you there, love, but Bell works at King Financial. It's not far from here."

I finished my slice and thanked Haithem.

"I have tickets to the Lied this weekend. I'd love for you to join me," he said, as we stood to leave.

"The Lied? That sounds great."

"But?"

"I've got to focus on this case."

"Well, how about you let me know where you are with things Saturday? The performance isn't until evening." He smiled. I sighed. God, how I love his accent.

"I'll let you know."

I left Haithem and headed to King Financial. It was a short walk. No sense moving my car and fighting for another parking spot. The receptionist greeted me, asked me to be seated, and phoned William Bell. After a few minutes, a lanky man with short dark hair and a goatee approached me. I stood to introduce myself.

"I was wondering if we could talk, privately?" I asked.

"Of course, follow me."

We entered a conference room off the main area. He closed the door and gestured to a seat. Bell sat at the head of the table. I handed him my card.

"How may I help you?"

"I'm curious how you might know a man by the name of Noble."

His eyes darted and his brow furrowed a bit. He sat up straighter and smoothed his slacks.

"I don't know anyone by that name. What's this about?"

"My client was engaged in a deal using Bitcoins. I understand that you trade them."

"But, how?"

It never ceases to amaze me how quickly people forget my job description.

"It's what I do. Your handle is Mr. Nobody."

His eyes widened.

"Look, I'm not all that interested in you. What I need to know is your connection to Noble. Why'd he back out?"

"I don't know what you're talking about. If you'll excuse me, I have a meeting." He stood.

"Mr. Bell, I get that you were the middle guy. Maybe you didn't know exactly what the trade was, or with whom, but I can tell you that there's a good reason why Noble backed off. You won't be able to hide from these people."

He returned to his seat.

"He works in our mail room sorting and delivering. One day, he noticed something on my desk about Bitcoins and asked me about it. He seemed really interested, so I started teaching him about the market."

"How did you set up the deal with Katmando?"

"James picked up on the trading side fast. I let him handle a few of my deals, then." Bell's gaze drifted to the windows.

"Mr. Bell?"

"He came to me with his idea. I told him no, but he kept bringing it up. And, I needed the money."

I thought Bell was well off. He was a senior accountant.

"I know what you're thinking." He returned his attention to me. "My youngest daughter was diagnosed with Leukemia. Insurance only covers so much." He shifted in his seat. "The bills were -- are -- piling up."

"So, Noble pulled out of the deal, disappeared, and if I'm understanding you correctly, he's got the money."

Bell shook his head, his eyes narrowed and his mouth tightened.

"Any idea where James Noble lives?"

"No. I checked the address on his application. It's a friend's."

"You went there?"

He nodded yes.

"That was stupid. Brave, but stupid."

*****

I left Bell's office with Noble's last known address. Back in my Jeep and ready to roll, my phone rang. I put the Jeep back into park.

"Dez Jackson."

"This is Katrina. What have you found out and where the hell have you been? I've been calling for the last hour."

I breathed deeply. It was meant to be one of those cleansing yoga breaths that calms you. You know the kind. It keeps you from rippin' someone a new asshole when they've gotten on your last nerve.

"Well?"

"Katrina, maybe you should consider smokin' some of that shit you sell. Investigations usually take longer than twenty-four hours to produce reliable information."

"You've got nothing, then."

"I didn't say that."

"Jesus, Dez. Don't fuck with me. I'm not in the mood."

"Clearly. I just met with a guy named William Bell. He's an accountant at King Financial."

"So?"

"Do you know a dealer named James Noble?"

"He's not one of mine."

"Has he ever been?"

"No. Is he the one? Where is he?"

"I don't know for sure. He was working at King Financial."

"With this Bell guy? Who's he?"

"Bell deals in Bitcoins. He was sort of training Noble."

"Where's Noble?"

"He was in Lincoln. I don't know if he still is. But, Katrina, he might not be the guy. I'm checking things out."

"He was part of Cane's crew."

"Edward Cane? I thought he was dead."

"He's a damn Phoenix. And, Dez, keep in touch."

Katrina told me how to find Cane. Getting a meeting with him was going to be a pain in the ass. There was only one person in Lincoln who I knew could make it happen on short notice — Pearley Santos. Back in the day, he trained in one of my parent's gyms. He won every amateur MMA fight in the area. We got close, but then his mom was killed. Never did find out what happened. After that, he dropped out of sight. Then, he started turning up in the news. Well, mug shots of him, anyway. He did some time. That's when he got hooked up with Edward Cane's crew. I scrolled through my list of contacts for his number. I wasn't sure it was the most current, but it was a start.

"Santos."

It's great to be Irish.

"Pearley, this is Dez."

Silence. I guess I should have expected that. It'd been a few years. Well, ten give or take.

"Dezeray Jackson?"

"Yeah, it's been a while. I know."

"A while?" He chuckled. "Last time I saw you, your ass was headed away from me, and the door slammed behind it."

"So, you remember, then?"

"You're difficult to forget, chica."

"How'v you been?"

"How about we dispense with the idle chit-chat. It's been too long, and we know each other too well. What do you want?"

"Fair enough. I need to talk to Cane."

"He's busy."

"I only need a few minutes."

"Why?"

"I'm looking for someone."

Silence.

"His name is Noble."

"What do you want with him?"

"Can't say."

"Can't help you."

Shit.

"He might have taken something from someone he shouldn't have."

"Who?"

"Katrina."

"Cane didn't sanction whatever it was."

"Then he won't get in the way?"

"No."

"Do you know where I can find Noble?"

"Check The Hood."

"Pearley?"

"What?"

"Thanks."

He hung up. Well, that went better than I expected.

*****

I headed to what the neighborhood locals affectionately called The Hood. It's an area from K to A streets and S. 27th to S. 9th streets. I heard that a gas station near S. 13th street was a hot spot, so I parked across the street, north of the building, and waited. The place was busy. Kids were in and out buying candy and sodas for about an hour, then traffic settled down a bit. I noticed a young guy, maybe in his 20s, hanging out along the side of the station. He fit the description the accountant gave me. He was wearing jeans, a black T-shirt, and red Converse All Stars. His hair was short, jet black and spiked. After a few minutes, he made a couple deals. I wasn't exactly sure how I was going to play this. The easiest plan was to make a purchase. I waited for his customers to walk away, then hopped out of my Jeep.

A late model brown, Impala careened around the corner to the west, and barreled in my direction. I dove toward my Jeep. The *pop, pop, pop,* was unmistakable. The smell of burnt rubber, smoke, and gas filled the air. The car sped away continuing north for a short distance before disappearing around a turn. I looked back to the gas station. People gathered around the body. I walked over, knowing what I would see. Whispers through the small crowd confirmed it was James Noble. Blood poured from his chest and mouth. Sirens blared in the distance. Time to go.

In my Jeep, I checked the time. It was almost 6 o'clock. Rush hour traffic would be manageable. I searched my console for a Lincoln phone directory and found Bell's address. It took me twenty minutes to get there. He lived on a tree-lined street with lots of shade. It would have been peaceful except for the flashing police and ambulance lights. Neighbors gathered behind yellow police tape. A body lay covered in the front yard. A folded newspaper was within reach of it.

I parked as close as possible to the scene, got out, and wandered over to the growing crowd. News crews were arriving. I found a spot near two women.

"What is Bridget going to do?" The woman with short brown hair said, as she wiped a tear from her face.

The second woman shook her head, unable to respond.

"Why would anyone want to hurt William?" The brown haired woman asked no one in particular.

"What happened?" I asked.

"Oh, it's just awful. That's William Bell under that tarp."

"Did you see what happened?"

"No, no. Thank God. I was inside. I live just there," she pointed across the street, opposite the William's home. "I heard something that sounded like a car backfiring. I checked through the window and saw William, there." She gestured to the body.

"Did you see the car?"

"Not really. I mean, I saw the back end, but that's all."

"Did you see the color?"

"I already told the police officers. Who are you?"

"Did you see the color?"

"Brown. I think it was brown."

I turned and walked away.

There wasn't anything left for me to do in Lincoln. Katrina made sure of that.

The drive home was long. Rather than stop at my place, I went to Easy Street.

"I need to see Karina." I told the bouncer at the door. It was early, so no line.

"She expecting you?"

"Probably not."

"Name?"

"Dez."

He used the radio on his shoulder to tell someone inside who I was.

"She's upstairs." He said as he opened the door.

I climbed the winding staircase to the upper level. The house lights were bright. Wait staff busied themselves with various chores to get ready for opening. I saw Katrina near the back, in the VIP section, sitting on a couch, sipping a martini.

"Dez, what brings you here? I think we're finished with that nasty bitcoin business."

"We need to talk. Privately."

She motioned for her guard to leave. I sat in a chair opposite her.

"You killed Noble and Bell."

She smiled.

"I get Noble, but why Bell?"

"Because."

I waited.

Realizing I wasn't going to say anything until she explained, Katrina set her drink onto the table between us.

"They stole from me."

"Noble stole from you."

"Bell helped."

"You don't know that. You don't know what he did. In fact, you don't know a fucking thing about him."

Her right eyebrow raised. "That doesn't matter. He stole from me and he was punished. Why the hell do you care so much about Bell?"

"He has - had a family. A sick daughter."

"We all have families. Some are sick. Some aren't."

I stood to leave.

"You and I are done."

She smiled, reached for her Martini, and sipped. She rested the glass on the arm of the couch, holding it by its stem, and leaned back, smiling.

"We'll see."

CHAPTER NINE

YELLOW BONES

I met Maxwell Hunter at the Magnolia Hotel in downtown Omaha. I'd never been inside the place, but if it was as magnificent as the outside, then I was ready to be impressed. As I approached the door, a porter opened it, allowing me to pass through. Hunter said he'd wait for me in the bar. I'd done my homework and knew I was looking for a light-skinned, bald, black male, about 5'11", with a lean build. He was just shy of 50 years old, with dimples and bluish-hazel eyes, according to the pictures. Hunter was single and never married. He'd made his money through a variety of business ventures, but mostly in quick-service restaurants. From behind the front desk, a petite woman, with brown hair styled into a pixie cut, greeted me. She directed me to the bar.

I spotted Maxwell Hunter sitting at a table in a corner furthest from the entrance. From his vantage point, he could see everyone. He was dressed casually in a stylish sport coat and stood as I approached the table.

"Ms. Jackson?"

"Mr. Hunter, it's a pleasure to finally put a face with the voice." I took a seat opposite his.

"Thank you for meeting me here. This is my first trip to Omaha. It's quite a city."

"It's changed a lot in recent years. Mostly for the better, I'd say."

"I might need to consider a few business opportunities here."

Hunter had contacted me a month ago. Since then, we'd had a handful of conversations about a woman he wanted to find. He'd started his search on Facebook. That allowed him to narrow the possibilities to a few states. He'd hired private investigators in each location. When I called saying I believed I'd found her, he scheduled this visit.

I reached into my leather satchel, retrieved a few surveillance photos, and slid them across the table to Hunter. He leaned forward. His long fingers, much like those of a pianist, sifted through the pictures. He picked one up and studied it, and then set it back onto the table.

"This is her."

"Are you sure? It's been a long time."

"Yes."

"What would you like me to do next?"

"Have you seen him?"

I reached into my bag, pulled out two more pictures, and placed them on top of the others.

"I believe that this is him," I said.

He peered down at the pictures, then shuffled them to compare the images with those of the woman. Lines formed across his brow. He pushed away from the table and breathed deeply as his left arm crossed in front of his body, and his right hand covered his mouth.

After several minutes, he said, "Keep watching her. I want to know everything about her. Where she works, who she's seeing. Everything. And, him." He pointed to the picture of the boy. "I want to know where he attends school, his activities. Everything."

"And, then?"

"Don't concern yourself with that, now. Get me the details."

I started gathering the pictures. He set his hand on top of them.

"I'll keep these." He slid them together, creating a neat pile. "This should cover your expenses for the time being. If not, then get back in touch." He'd removed an envelope from his inside breast pocket and handed it to me. I glanced inside. Trust, but verify -- that's my motto.

"Okay. Should I update you via email, text, or phone?"

"Phone."

I stood to leave. We shook hands, and I left him, sitting there, staring at the pictures. I glanced back. A tear slid down his cheek. He swiped it away.

*****

Lisa Banks lived in the Fairacres neighborhood of what is now known as Midtown Omaha. She and her husband owned a brick house that sat far back from the road. A manicured lawn sprawled in front of it. All I could think was, "I'd hate to have to mow that." Of course, that thought was followed by, "They probably don't." The exterior brick had been painted white at one time. Now it had that faded, old-world charm. A driveway curved around the lawn, to the front doors, and continued around the other side. It was wide and accommodated entry or exit from either side. The house rested atop a hill. Semicircular steps led to red-painted double doors.

I parked along the street waiting for Lisa to leave. After a month of surveillance, I had her schedule memorized. Monday through Friday, she left the house at 9 o'clock a.m. She and a female partner owned a day spa in Rockbrook Village. Her partner's name was Rebecca Dupont. Both women were in their mid-30s and married to wealthy men, who were in their 50s. Their husbands didn't work together, but they all socialized in the same tight circle of old money millionaires.

Her son attended Central High School. I wasn't clear what went into that decision. Don't get me wrong, there's nothing wrong with Central High School, I just couldn't figure out why a millionaire would send his son there. Or, why a millionaire's wife would. It seems to me they'd send him to a private school like Brownell-Talbot. Who knows why millionaires do what they do with their money? They're an odd bunch. And, in my experience so far, this family wasn't any different. Their son's name is Thomas Banks, but his friends and mother call him Tommy. I'd planned to check in on him later today, but for now, I wanted to see what Marjory was up to.

I followed her Mercedes through the northside streets of Midtown, crossed over Dodge Street, the dividing line between north and south in Omaha, and continued to Center Street. Rockbrook Village is located on Elm Street, just south of Center Street and east of the 680 Interstate. I parked my black Jeep several spaces from the spa and waited about five minutes before following her inside. In the month since I'd been observing her, I'd never entered the spa, but today, I wanted to get a better feel for her personality.

The lavender-perfumed air assaulted my nose the moment I walked through the doors. A little goes a long way, and it seemed that these people wanted their guests to pass out upon entry. A young woman, probably in her mid-20s, with flawless skin, smiled at me from behind a long desk. The entryway was painted in soft hues of yellow and pink. Plush couches lined the walls to the left. Fashion magazines adorned an L-shaped, wood coffee table. To my right, there was a champagne and wine bar. Beyond that, a glass wall divided the entryway from a room where guests were engaged in yoga poses. A series of doors fed off of a main hall to me left just past the waiting area. Signs on the doors indicated when the room was occupied.

"How may I help you?"

"I would love to get a facial. Oh, it's been ages since I had one," I said. Actually, it was more like never, but she didn't need to know that.

"Normally, you'd need an appointment, but we happen to have a cancellation. Cynthia will be able to help you in a few minutes. I'll let her know that she has a guest. Please, enjoy a complimentary glass of wine or champagne while you wait."

I thanked her and headed to the bar. A free glass of wine sounded pretty appealing. I sat on a cushy stool sipping a glass of Merlot when I spotted Lisa. She was in the hall, outside of the yoga room, talking with her partner. By the expression on her face, I got the impression that something was wrong. I grabbed my drink and walked down the hall, slowing as I passed them, and pretended to watch the class.

"Lisa, this is getting out of hand. We can't continue that portion of our business. I don't want anything to do with it."

I saw Lisa glance my direction.

"Keep your voice down. Let's go into my office and discuss it." The two women disappeared around the corner at the end of the hall. I returned to the front, dropped off my half-empty glass, and left.

*****

That conversation got me curious. What had her partner meant? I gave it a little thought as I sat in afternoon traffic on West Dodge Road, trying to make my way over to Zio's Pizzeria. Sure, I could have stopped at the one on Center Street, but it didn't have the same feel as the original spot. I thought I'd done my due diligence researching her spa, but maybe I missed something. Traffic started moving and I was able to see the holdup. A construction crew was blocking off two of the eastbound lanes just past 90th Street. Luckily, Zio's wasn't too far off from there. The lot was full. I had to circle a few times and wait for someone to leave, but the pizza is worth it.

As I entered Zio's the aroma of fresh-made dough and sauce wafted through the air. I inhaled. A smile spread across my face. It was crowded, but the wait was only 15 minutes. I ordered a soda and stared at the TV in the floor. Who doesn't like cartoons in the afternoon?

I got a table near the windows, ordered two slices of cheese with mushrooms, a side salad, and a beer. My phone vibrated on the table. It was Haithem Nazari. He was in Omaha and wanted to meet up for lunch. Ten minutes later he sat across from me. I brought him up to speed on my current case.

"So, what do you think she was talking about?" he asked, and took a bite of his slice.

"I'm not sure. I didn't find anything that would make me believe it was anything other than an ordinary spa. Well, except that it's only for women. I suppose that makes it a bit different."

"They don't have any services for men?"

"None."

"I feel slighted." Haithem grinned.

"I'm sure you do." I finished my second slice and my beer. "There is one other thing that's sort of different about the place."

"What's that?"

"For a women's spa, there aren't a lot of women working there. Every time I've watched the place, I've seen young men, mostly in their 20s entering. They're all in great shape. Model material, really. There are two college-age women working the front desk. One of them also handles walk-ins."

"You've been watching the spa for a month?"

"Yeah."

"Maybe that's just part of their business model. Something like Hooters."

"Yeah, maybe, but it's all I have to go on at the moment."

We finished lunch. Haithem had a meeting at The Lab. It's the scientific research arm of Tracer International. The office in Lincoln handles basic analysis and anything tech-related, but The Lab is on par with FBI Laboratory Services in Quantico, VA. I had a little more research to do on the spa, but also wanted to get downtown. Tommy Banks was getting out of school, soon, and I wanted to see what he was up to. We said our usual good-byes, with me promising to take him up on his dinner offer. It wasn't that I wasn't attracted to Haithem. I just wasn't in the right frame of mind for a relationship with a former coworker.

From Zio's I headed east to the one area of town where I knew I'd get a WIFI connection without leaving the comfort of my Jeep -- Aksarben Village. The Village is a mixture of University of Nebraska-Omaha campus housing and departments, hotels, retail businesses, office space, and a park complete with an outdoor stage. I heard that Zumba classes are taught on Sundays during the summer, but I haven't managed to get up for any of them. It's not that the park is far from my place; it's about a 10-minute drive in traffic, but I figured if I wanted to dance with strangers, I could go to a club.

I parked on Mercy Road on the north side of Stinson Park. With my tablet resting on the passenger seat, I conducted a series of searches about Lisa's spa. The only thing of note was the grand opening several years ago. The chamber of commerce conducted a ribbon-cutting. The story was in the Midlands Business Journal. For a rich lady, her business wasn't very philanthropic. There were no benefits or giveaways. No specials. And, no other news coverage in The Omaha World-Herald, The Reader, or any other major or minor print medium. I checked to see whether her business maintained a chamber membership. It looked like she dropped it a few years after the business opened. Of course, with her husband's and partner's connections, she probably didn't believe she needed the chamber.

I clicked open a file with her name and reviewed my notes from the past month. As I scrolled through the pages, I found a list of people in Nebraska having her last name. Initially, I'd

DEADLY SINS · 147

thought maybe she changed her first name, or was going by a middle name, and planned to check these people out, but then I got a hit on a Lisa G. Banks, and rolled with it. Sometimes, I get lucky. I like to believe it's because I'm Irish. Near the bottom of the list, there were two women listed whose names were Beth Geoffreys. One lived in Omaha, and the other in some small town in Nebraska that I'd never heard of, and probably didn't want to visit. Maybe Lisa showing up in Omaha had something to do with her having a relative here. Maybe it wasn't a random decision.

Beth Geoffreys lived in north Omaha in the Ponca Hills neighborhood. The drive over would have taken 20 minutes if I hadn't gotten slowed down by an accident on 72nd Street just before Blondo. Ponca Hills is north of I-680. The neighborhood stretches west to Highway 75 and north to the Douglas/Washington County line and is mostly hilly terrain with a blend of wilderness, parks, agriculture and family homes. If I lived over here, I'd be hiking the trails in Hummel, Dodge, or Neale Park every day.

Mrs. Geoffreys lived in a ranch-style, brick house with a well-maintained front yard. My guess was that someone handled the outside chores for her. According to what I'd researched, she was at least 75 years old. I parked on the street. It's always good practice to have more than one way to leave. Driveways are a trap. I walked the paved path to the front door and rang the bell. I hadn't called ahead because I couldn't locate a number matching the address. That was kind of a pain in the ass, if I was way off base with this hunch. No one answered. I rang the bell a few more times and waited. As I returned to my car, I thought I heard someone singing. It was coming from the north side of the house. I walked over and peeked around the corner. A petite woman, wearing a wide-brimmed hat, long pants and a short-sleeved T-shirt, crouched among rose bushes, trimming dead branches. She flung one behind her, almost hitting me. I jumped aside, landed on a pile of landscape rock next to the house, started slipping, but the house stopped me from falling on my ass. Mrs. Geoffreys stood up to face me, shears in hand, poised to attack.

"Shit!" she said. "Who the hell are you?"

I composed myself, stepped from the mound of rocks, and extended my hand with my business card. She took it.

"Private investigator? What do I want with a private investigator?"

"Actually, I have a few questions. I'm looking for a woman to whom you might be related."

"All my relations are either dead, or should be."

"Do you happen to know a woman named Lisa Geoffreys Banks?"

Mrs. Geoffreys tossed the shears to the ground. "Let's go inside. I need a break. Damn roses. I should've planted a friggin' evergreen row."

I followed Mrs. Geoffreys around to the back. We entered the house through a door off of the kitchen. I thought I had stepped onto the set of "Leave it to Beaver." She invited me to sit. I pulled out a metal chair with a red, vinyl seat cover. She set two glasses of water onto the table, along with a bottle of scotch and two empty glasses. She sat opposite me.

"At my age, it keeps my heart hummin' along." She poured a finger of scotch into one glass, and then offered some to me. I was tempted, but it wasn't even 5 o'clock, yet. The thought hadn't fully formed when she said, "It's 5 o'clock somewhere. Live a little."

I nodded. She filled my glass.

"Lisa Geoffreys Banks, you say?"

"Uh, huh." I took a sip of the Maker's Mark.

"Well, I have a granddaughter by that name minus the Banks."

I retrieved a picture of Lisa from my satchel and slid it across the table to her. She picked up the photo, studied it for a few seconds, and then dropped it onto the table.

"That's her."

*****

Apparently, it was easy to lose touch with relatives in a city the size of Omaha because she hadn't seen Tommy Banks since he was 5 years old. Twelve years ago, Lisa showed up on her doorstep, from Atlanta or wherever, and demanded that Mrs. Geoffreys help her, since she never helped Lisa's mother. After a few months, Lisa was gone. No explanation. No "thank you." Nothing. She took Tommy and left. I'd shown Mrs. Geoffrey's a few pictures I had, and let her keep a few of Tommy. When she saw them, she remarked that it was good that he still passed. "That probably made things easier for him," she said.

After meeting with Mrs. Geoffreys, I headed in the direction of Central High School. I'd told Maxwell Hunter that I'd get more information about Tommy's plans after graduation. I planned to speak with his guidance counselor, but hadn't quite worked out my lie. I might take the recruiter approach.

I drove south on 30th Street, noticing how much the neighborhood had changed. One of the Catholic schools had closed. Miller Park pool was smaller. The city had changed it into a kiddie pool. There weren't many businesses until I passed Metropolitan Community College-Fort Omaha campus. And, Mr. C's had closed years before I returned to Omaha. It was Christmas year round in that place when I was a kid. My parents loved Italian food and dragged us to every Italian eatery in Omaha. Mr. C's and Lo Sole Mio were my favorites.

I arrived at Central High School, downtown, via 20th Street and went around the block to 24th Street, then turned east on Davenport Street to reach the back of Central High School. An ambulance was parked in a lot outside of the stadium. I parked in an empty spot, which was probably for a teacher, but since it was empty, I figured that they didn't need it. Then, I grabbed my satchel, got out, and walked past the ambulance. As I approached the back doors, the EMTs rushed out with their gurney. I stepped out of the way. My eyes followed the action. Tommy Banks, face contorted and bloody, lay strapped to the gurney. I made a beeline for my Jeep, waited for them to leave, and followed the ambulance through town. They were headed to the University of Nebraska Medical Center on 43rd and Dewey Avenue.

I waited a few minutes before going inside the emergency room. It was packed. I found a spot near the patient entrance. A few minutes later, I slipped inside the ER and searched for Tommy Banks. I located him. He was out cold. His chart rested on a table near him. I thumbed through it, grabbed my phone, and snapped a few pictures. Then I snagged a few hairs from his head, tucked them inside a baggie I kept in my satchel - 'cause you never know when you're going to need one - and sneaked back out. There was so much going on, no one noticed me. Which is a damn good thing since going to jail wasn't on my agenda for the afternoon.

Safe inside my Jeep, I reviewed the images of Tommy's chart. He had a few broken ribs, a broken nose, and was missing a few teeth. The doctors had sedated him. He was going to live, but be in a lot of pain for a little while. I called Haithem to ask if I could drop the hair sample at The Lab. He said he'd make the necessary arrangements, so I made my way over there.

*****

There are only two ways into The Lab, and I didn't have clearance for either one. I waited outside a metal door at the front of the building. A small camera, mounted to the wall to my right, announced my presence. The intercom crackled and a disembodied voice asked for my name. A few seconds later, the metal door unlocked and opened. I entered an alcove surrounded by glass walls. There were two cameras mounted to the walls to my left and right. The metal door clanged shut. A hallway stretched from the alcove to a far wall. It was easily one hundred feet. Other hallways extended from the main. A short, older man appeared from around the corner at the end of the hall. Beneath his white lab coat, his clothes were disheveled, as was his hair. He hurried to greet me. Still trapped in the alcove, I smiled and waved.

"Dezeray Jackson, it's a pleasure to finally meet you." He scanned his security card in front of a reader on the wall to his left. The wall in front of me slid open. I stepped into the hall. The wall slid closed. "Do you have the sample?"

I reached into my jacket pocket, pulled out the little baggie, and handed it to him.

"I'm sorry, but I didn't catch your name."

"Oh, so sorry! Where are my manners? I'm Dr. Drake. William Drake." We shook hands. "This shouldn't take too long to process. Would you like to wait?"

"That would be great, thanks."

I followed Dr. Drake through a series of interconnected hallways that eventually opened into a large, fully enclosed lab surrounded and divided by glass walls. Within each section, researchers busied themselves with their projects.

"If you'll just wait right here a moment." He scanned his security card and entered The Lab. I watched as he passed several other research areas before turning into his section. Everything they did here was a mystery to me. All I cared about was that they always found the answers. I wasn't sure how long I'd be waiting, so I grabbed my phone and played Fruit Ninja. When I got bored with that, I moved on to Angry Birds. Twenty minutes later, Dr. Drake reappeared.

"Here you go." He handed me the report for Tommy Banks' hair.

I scanned the analysis and then asked, "What exactly am I seeing here?"

"What do you mean?"

"Well, if I'm understanding this correctly, this person is black."

"Yes, that's correct. It looks like he's biracial. Is that what you needed to know?"

"Yes, thank you."

"If there isn't anything else that you need, I'll escort you to the main door."

"No, this is all I need."

*****

It was nearly 5 o'clock, which meant I was going to get caught up in traffic. There wasn't any reason for me to rush to find Lisa; she'd be with Tommy at the hospital, and that wasn't the ideal place for me to confront her about who his father is. I wasn't even sure Tommy knew. I called Maxwell Hunter and gave him the good news before heading to Brazenhead Irish Pub, off of 78th and Dodge Streets. Happy Hour wasn't over and I heard Guinness calling my name.

When I arrived at the pub, I found a spot at the back bar, and ordered a Brian Boru Boxty, and of course, a Guinness. A band started up around 7 p.m. A couple of college guys joined me and struck up a conversation. That led to a scotch and a few more rounds of Guinness. It turned out they were from Dublin. I ended up staying until reverse happy hour started. I might have stayed longer, but I could sense that the guys were feeling a bit too cozy with me. I said my goodbyes and headed home. I figured Godfrey would be pretty ticked off at me for leaving him alone in the house most of the day, so I'd ordered a plain burger to go.

*****

The next morning, proof in hand, I decided to head over to the spa and talk with Banks. I arrived at the spa as she was opening up.

"Lisa Banks?"

She turned to face me.

"Yes, may I help you?"

"We need to talk. Do you mind if we step inside?"

"What's this about?"

"Your son, Tommy."

She opened the door and I followed her inside.

"Give me a minute. I need to turn a few things on."

Banks left me in the lobby area as she turned on lights and music. The place still smelled of lavender. After about five minutes, she returned to the front.

"What about my son?"

"I work for a man named Maxwell Hunter."

The color drained from her face.

"I don't know anyone by that name."

I handed her a copy of the DNA analysis. She looked it over and gave it back.

"Is that supposed to mean something to me?"

"I know Tommy is Maxwell Hunter's son. And, so does he."

"This is ridiculous. How do you even know my son?"

"I'm a private investigator. Hunter hired me to find you."

She began pacing in front of the reception desk.

"Then it was him!"

"What are you talking about?"

"Someone attacked my son yesterday."

"Maxwell Hunter didn't attack your son. That makes no sense."

"Then he hired someone to do it."

"What makes you think it was anything more than a fight?"

"How do you know he had a fight?"

"It's kind of in my job description."

"Oh, right. My son hasn't ever gotten into a fight. He was attacked and if it doesn't have anything to do with Maxwell, then I need to know who it was."

"So, you do know Mr. Hunter, then."

"What? Okay, yes, I do know him, but it's been a very long time."

"Yes, about 17 years by my calculations."

"Maxwell and I had a relationship when I was a freshman in college. It didn't last. I moved on. He apparently did not. He has nothing to do with my son. You tell him that if he comes near me or my son, I'll have him arrested."

"Hmm, okay, but he has a right to see his son, so I'm not exactly clear how you'd have him arrested. Listen, all he wants is a chance to meet him. He's not asking for anything else."

She continued pacing.

"Right now, I'm more concerned about who hurt my son. Maybe you could make yourself more useful by finding that out. Surely Maxwell has an interest in that, too. You must have told him what happened."

"I did, and yes, he's concerned."

"Then go do that."

"What about Mr. Hunter's request?"

"Tommy doesn't know anything about Maxwell."

"So, Tommy doesn't know that he's biracial?"

"No, and it needs to stay that way. Please, just find out who attacked my son. I'll figure out something to satisfy Maxwell's curiosity."

*****

After I left Lisa Banks' spa, I called Maxwell Hunter to fill him in on where I was with the case. He agreed that I should help Lisa find out more about the attack on Tommy. My next call was to Officer Jacobs. He'd helped me with a few personal issues at my property a while back, and I knew he worked the downtown area. He said the two guys who jumped Tommy Banks disappeared. The description from witnesses was that the guys were white, early 20s, and probably skinheads. Police were investigating areas known as hangouts for white supremacist groups, but so far, the two guys hadn't surfaced.

I wondered why white supremacists would attack a white kid, or at least, one who looked white. Was it some weird initiation? Other gangs do that sort of thing. I'd barely finished my thought when Officer Jacobs confirmed it. The investigating officers believed it was an initiation, but they couldn't speak with Tommy Banks, yet. He was still sedated. I thanked Officer Jacobs for his help, and decided to ask the one person who I knew would know about white supremacist activity in Omaha. It was a bit early for Eddy's to be open, but Eddy was always there. He lived above the pool hall.

Fifteen minutes later, I stood outside the pool hall entrance and rang the buzzer for Eddy's place. He said he'd meet me around back at the kitchen entrance. I left my Jeep parked in front and walked around the building. Eddy opened the metal, windowless door.

"What's up?" he asked as I entered. The door slammed shut behind me.

"What's the occasion?" I asked, and followed him through the small kitchen into the main pool hall.

"Oh, this old thing?" He gestured to his tailored gray, pinstriped suit. "I'm meeting with a potential business partner."

"Ah. Hey, I'm curious about local white supremacist activity."

"Curious? Why?"

We sat at a table in the bar. Eddy's still was the only place to get a decent game. And, by decent, I mean lucrative. Eddy grew up in Omaha during the late 40s, joined the navy, and returned in the 60s. He knew about everyone and everything worth knowing in Omaha.

"I know a kid who got jumped, and I'm trying to figure out the Ws of the situation."

"I'm guessin' you already know the where."

"Yeah. I need more information about who, what, and why. The police think it's some kind of initiation."

"Is your kid black, brown, or white?"

"White. And rich. He's a senior at Central."

"There's been a lot of activity downtown, mostly to the east, near the river."

"What kind of activity?"

"Black kid got jumped by five skinheads for crossing into the wrong part of CB a few weeks back. He wasn't from here. Apparently, he didn't get the 'do not cross' memo. A couple nights ago, there was a house fire. You probably heard about that one. It'll all settle back down after Obama is gone and another white dude gets elected." Eddy grabbed a handful of trail mix from a bowl on the counter.

CB was what people from Omaha called Council Bluffs. It's a town in Iowa just across the Missouri River.

"That the one with the biracial kid?"

"That's the one."

The family's garage was decorated with swastikas. You'd think CB was a no-man's land if you weren't white, but a few neighbors got together and covered the garage. It couldn't be painted because it was an on-going investigation.

"There's been more ever since the Brown case. Some folks feel a need to prove their solidarity with that cop."

Eddy was referring to the Michael Brown killing in Missouri. Omaha hadn't seen anything like that clash, but it got lots of locals into the streets, protesting. That alone was enough to spark backlash from a few white supremacists.

"A few nights ago, a couple young skins came in here. Never seen them before. Lots of money to spend."

"You remember anything else about them?"

"My new girl mentioned they were wearing black Celtic crosses. She hadn't seen that before."

"New girl?"

"Misty. She started last week."

"Why would two skinheads come into your place? They had to know they'd be in mixed company."

"They came to play. Misty said they were up a few hundred when they left."

"How long were they around?"

"A few hours. Misty might know more. She was interested in one of them. She ain't got a lick of sense when it comes to men. She's always attracted to the badass. She don't care what color he is."

"How do I get in contact with Misty?"

"She lives with her mother down off of Minne Lusa not too far from the park. You remember The Viking Ship building?"

"Yeah."

"Her place is a few houses north of that on the west side of the street."

*****

Misty wasn't home when I got to her place, but her mother was. She answered the door in a pale-blue bathrobe. Her hair fell over the front of her shoulders. A cigarette dangled from her lips. She held a glass in her left hand as she stood behind the screened door. I introduced myself.

"I don't know where the hell she is." She snubbed out her cigarette and lit another one. It was her second in the two minutes since I'd arrived. "She met some guy the other night, that's all I know. They came back here after she got off work, and were fuckin' so loud, I didn't get any sleep. Told them both to leave."

"Any chance you know the guy's name, or what he looked like?"

"What the fuck do I care?"

"Anything at all?"

She sucked on her third cigarette, blew out the smoke, and drained the contents of the glass. The familiar aroma of bad scotch wafted through the screened door.

"Stupid fuck had a swastika on his ass."

"Okay, that's helpful. Ya know, if I happen to see him naked. Can you think of anything else? What color was his hair?"

"He didn't have much, but it was probably brown."

"Was he taller than you?"

"No, he was more like my height."

"You're what? About 5'7"?

"Yeah, how'd you know?"

"Lucky guess. Can you think of where Misty might have gone? I'm thinking they came here because they couldn't go to his place."

"She's got a friend named Cari. She lives a few blocks from here."

I got the address and left. Cari's house was on Newport Street, up near 24th Street. When I got there, I passed a car idling opposite the house. A young guy, with short blonde hair, sat in the driver's seat smoking a cigarette. I continued east on Newport a half block before turning around and parking. A guy stepped out of the house, backwards. A girl, who I figured was Misty, wrapped her hands around his neck as he struggled to tuck in his shirt. I got a flash of butt-crack and swastika tattoo. Shirt tucked, and hands free, he pulled her hands off and turned away. He wandered over to the waiting car and got into the passenger side. I made a note of the license plate. They were driving a late model Camaro. The driver headed east on Newport. I turned my Jeep around and followed.

As they made their way through north Omaha neighborhoods to the lower east side, I realized where they were going, and it wasn't anywhere I wanted to be. Confronting them on their own ground wasn't a good idea. They pulled up to a little shack of a place and disappeared inside. Motorcycles lined the gravel lot. I found a spot on the street. I'd have to wait it out. Forty minutes later, the guys reappeared, got into the Camaro, and drove west and then south. They were heading downtown. Neutral territory. They parked in The Old Market, got out of the car, and walked in the direction of Spaghetti Works. I rounded the block, got lucky, and found someone pulling out of spot.

Some things don't change. When I was a teen, the skinheads gathered in the same spot as these guys. They were alone when I approached them near one of the large street planters. I handed each of them my business card. They couldn't have been more than 22 or 23 years old. They read my card, and then the one with a tat on his ass, flicked it to the ground. A crooked grin formed at the corner of his mouth. I ignored it and jump-started the conversation.

"I have a hunch that if I show your pictures to a certain young man, that he'll ID you as the ones who jumped him. What I want to know is who told you to target him."

"We ain't got nothin' to say to you, bitch," Tat-Ass said.

"Okay, then we'll do this the hard way. I'll call the cops, who we all know have been looking for you, and I'll tell them what you're driving, including your plate. Then I'll show them the pictures I snapped of you coming out of Cari's place, and you sitting in the car. I'm sure they already know about the shantytown shack in east O. Finding you should be a piece of cake after that."

The blonde shifted his stance. The other one stepped up to me.

"Seriously, you're too young and too pretty to do time," I said to the blonde. "And you," I said, turning my attention back to Tat-Ass. "Really should back off."

"Come on man, sit down. She ain't really got nothin' on us."

"Oh, I have plenty to get this ball rollin' in your direction. But, like I said, I'm only interested in why you targeted that kid."

The blonde fidgeted and shoved his hands into his jacket pockets.

"The way I hear it, hate crimes are getting treated pretty serious these days. The OPD doesn't want to make national news for the wrong reasons. I'll just give my buddy, Officer Jacobs a call, and have him meet me down here. They figured it was some sort of an initiation or something. Anyway, they're probably right." I shrugged my shoulders and turned to walk away.

"It wasn't," the blonde shouted.

I stopped in my tracks and turned back to face them.

"It wasn't, what?"

"An initiation."

"Do tell."

"Some lady paid us to jump that kid."

"Shut up, man!" Tat-Ass punched the blonde in the shoulder.

"Fuck you, I ain't goin' to prison over this shit." The blonde stood up.

"What lady?" I asked.

"Hicks. Marjory Hicks."

"And how did Marjory Hicks get in touch with two upstanding guys like you?"

"We clean her pool."

"Why did she hire you?"

"She said she wanted to send some other lady a message. That's all we know."

Tat-Ass sat on the planter, lit a cigarette, and glared at me.

"You're not going to turn us in, right?" The blonde actually looked hopeful. He needed to re-think his devotion to the cause, that's for sure.

"Yeah, yeah. No problem. Like I said, I just needed some information. The police can figure this out on their own. It's why they get paid the big bucks."

I left the two dipshits to their musings. Before leaving The Old Market, I called Officer Jacobs and gave him the information about Tat-Ass and Blondey. Then, I located an address for Marjory Hicks. What I knew about her, from various news sources, was that she had new money, no career ambitions, and a lot of time for socializing. Why would she hire two thugs to beat up Tommy Banks?

*****

Marjorie Hicks answered the door of her McMansion, which to be honest, surprised me. I sort of expected to see a servant. I introduced myself. She didn't invite me inside.

"I don't know how I could possibly help you."

"Let's just cut to the chase, all right? I'm a bit pressed for time. You hired two guys to jump Lisa Banks' son. I want to know why. At least, ya know, before I tell the police."

She didn't even flinch. How many people do you know wouldn't flinch when the police are mentioned alongside their name?

"I've got an appointment." She started to shut the door. I slid my foot between it and the frame.

"Okay, clearly you didn't hear what I said. Your two pool guys gave you up. When I show their pictures to Tommy Banks, he'll positively ID them. Then, they'll throw you under the bus to save their asses. Now, you and I both know that you'll get off, but not without it making a few headlines first."

"Come in."

I followed her into a large foyer, past a spiral staircase, and into a spacious living room.

"Please, sit down. Would you like a beverage?"

Wow. This was new. It's rare to witness a person change her tune so abruptly, but I gotta say, I like it when it's in my favor.

"I'm good, thanks. About Tommy Banks,"

"It's not about Tommy. I just needed to get her attention."

"Her?"

"Lisa. Her spa isn't exactly a spa."

"You're going to have to spell this out for me."

Marjorie Hicks' smoothed her pant legs, sat forward in her seat, and took a deep breath.

"Lisa's spa provides women with services that they may not otherwise receive in their marriages. Usually, discreetly."

"I see. So what happened?"

"I learned that she was keeping a list of her better-off customers and the services they required."

"And, your name is on that list?"

She nodded.

"You confronted Lisa?"

"Yes. When she refused to destroy the list, I knew I had to make a stronger appeal to her sense of right and wrong."

"Those two guys you hired did a number on Tommy. He's still in the hospital."

"I had no idea what they'd do. I simply asked that they give him a message to deliver to his mother."

"Well, I guess you can consider the message delivered."
*****

After leaving Hicks' place, I called Maxwell Hunter to let him know what I'd discovered. Then I returned to the spa. I arrived before closing. The young lady at the front desk directed me to Lisa's office.

"Lisa, why don't you tell me a bit more about your business?"

She was seated behind a glass-topped desk. Her office was devoid of family pictures or keepsakes of any kind. I noticed a few small boxes in a corner. I sat opposite her. The desktop was empty, except for a phone.

"You already know everything about it."

"I don't think so. See, I just had a chat with a woman named Marjorie Hicks. I believe you might know her." Small wrinkles formed at the corner of Lisa's mouth. "I can see that you're familiar with that name. Anyhoo, she mentioned that you operate an interesting side business for your more well-off clients."

"I don't know what she's talking about. This is a spa. Occasionally, our guests require a little something extra, and my staff are willing to provide those things, but there's nothing unusual about that."

"Mrs. Hicks was concerned about a list you're keeping on those not-so-unusual requests."

"She's the one who sent those thugs to attack Tommy?"

"Afraid so. I have to say that I think you're out of your league, here. Hicks's husband is more connected than yours, she has access to more money, and she's accustomed to getting what she wants. Why not just destroy the list?"

Lisa stood, grabbed her jacket and her purse.

"It's my insurance policy."

"I got that, but it put your son into the hospital. Next time, he might not be so lucky."

"Tommy graduates in two weeks. After that, he's going on holiday, and then straight to university. She won't be able to find him."

"Don't the schools usually announce where the seniors are going?"

"He was undecided when all of that was needed, so the school doesn't have the information."

"Then, she might step it up, and send someone after you."

"I know. I can live with that."

"Mr. Hunter wants to make arrangements to see Tommy."

She brushed past me and picked up the boxes.

"He has a right to see him."

"I'll tell Tommy about Maxwell after graduation. If Tommy wants to meet him, then he can decide. Tell Maxwell that." She walked out of the office, but stopped short. "Tell Maxwell to leave."

I watched her walk down the hallway and disappear around the corner. I called Hunter to tell him Lisa was leaving, and that I was going to the Banks' house. Lisa had a history of bolting when things got messy. Her grandmother confirmed that. With Tommy about to graduate, and Marjorie Hicks causing trouble, Lisa had no reason to stay. She didn't need her husband's money. With her list, she could live off of her future blackmail demands.

When I arrived at the Banks' house, the front door was open, and I could hear the raised voices of two men. I recognized one as Maxwell Hunter. I entered the home and followed the sound to a living room. Tommy Banks reclined on a couch. Maxwell Hunter stood with his back to the entrance of the room, and Mr. Banks stood in front of the couch.

"Who are you?" Mr. Banks redirected his anger to me.

"I'm Dezeray Jackson."

"She's the investigator I hired to find Lisa and my son," Hunter said. "You can't ignore the evidence!"

"Tommy is my son. Clearly, there's been a mistake. He's white. You're colored."

The room became very quiet. Maxwell Hunter spoke, again, in measured tones.

"The DNA report is accurate. If need be, we'll run another test. Tommy is my son."

Tommy struggled to stand. It was clear that the pain from his broken ribs made it difficult. He winced and almost stumbled back onto the couch. Banks caught Tommy's shoulders and steadied him.

"Dad? What's he talking about?"

Banks stared at Tommy, and then returned his attention to the report Maxwell had apparently given him before I arrived. Tommy peered over his father's shoulder and looked at the report.

"But, I'm not colored. Mom said my father was white. She told me he died in an accident. That's why we left Atlanta."

"She lied to you," I said. "Do you remember your grandmother, Beth?"

"No, not really."

"She'll tell you that Mr. Hunter is telling you the truth. And as he's already said, we can get another test, but I can assure you that The Lab doesn't make mistakes."

Mr. Banks dropped the report onto a table next to the couch.

"He can't be my son."

"Dad?"

Banks walked to a nearby bar, poured himself a drink, and took a big gulp.

"I realize that this is a shock for everyone, but Mr. Banks, you've been Tommy's father for the last 12 or 13 years. You're the only father he's known. And while Mr. Hunter has a right to pursue this legally, it would be best if you could come to some sort of agreement."

"He can't be my son!" Banks slammed his glass onto the bar and turned back to face us. "I can't have a nigger for a son."

The color drained from Tommy's face. I thought he might throw up. He snatched up the report and left the room. I could hear his heavy steps as he climbed the stairs near the entryway.

"What the fuck is wrong with you?" The words left my mouth before I realized what I was saying.

Hunter shot me a side glance. Banks seemed startled by the ferocity of my voice.

"What are you going to do? Desert him? You do understand that Lisa isn't coming back, right? You raised him to be just like you. Do you have any idea how fucked up that is?" I asked. "And now, you want to walk away?"

"Banks, we're going to have to put our differences aside so we can help Tommy. Whether I like it or not, you're his father. Even if you're a racist, bigoted fool."

"You two need to leave."

"Here's my contact information. Please ensure that Tommy receives it. I'm staying in Omaha for the next several weeks." Hunter laid his business card onto the table. "We need to handle this carefully. The boy is confused and angry." He paused, and then added, "And hurt."

"You're presence here doesn't help that."

I placed my card next to Hunter's, along with Beth Geoffreys' phone number.

"I'll be keeping an eye on Tommy for a while longer."

"That isn't necessary."

"Yes, I think it is. Lisa got herself into a little bind. The person who had Tommy attacked might do it, again."

"I can take care of Tommy."

"Right. I think that might be a bit challenging considering what you just told him. Chances are, he's upstairs packing."

"I didn't mean ..."

"Yes, you did. And he knows it."

Hunter and I left the Banks' house. I felt for Tommy. He'd been lied to his entire life, and now his whole world had changed in an instant. He would always pass for white, but the question was, would he still want to? Could Banks ever accept Tommy, now that they knew the truth? Hunter seemed oddly quiet as we walked to our cars.

"Mr. Hunter?"

We stopped in front of his rental car.

"I have all of the information I need. Thank you."

"Do you want me to track Lisa?"

"No. She'll turn up eventually. Now I only want a chance to get to know Tommy. You said that he's going on holiday after graduation?"

"Yes. He's doing a tour of Great Britain." I'd discovered that while doing a few background checks on Lisa a few months ago.

"And, what university is he planning to attend?"

"Loyola."

"Well, I guess all I can do now, is wait. I'm used to that."

"At least he knows."

He smiled. It was forced.

"Here," he said, and handed me a large manila envelope. Then he shook his head, shrugged, and got into his car. I watched as he drove away. Back inside my Jeep, I opened the envelope. It had a final payment for services, and two smaller envelopes. The first was to me. The second was addressed to Tommy.

Mine read: Please give this to Tommy. I established a college fund for him years ago, and another account just because. He can access both when he turns 18.

I got back out of my car, and returned to the Banks' house. Tommy had just opened the door. I saw two suitcases and a backpack on the floor, behind him. Mr. Banks stood at the base of the stairs. He'd been saying something about not meaning what he'd said.

"This is for you."

"What is it?"

"It's from Maxwell."

Tommy opened the envelope, read the note, and looked back at me.

"Where are you headed?" I asked.

"Anywhere, but here."

"Need a ride?"

"Yeah, that'd be great. Thanks."

I let him pass me and walked inside to get his bags. Banks stood motionless.

"You know how to reach me," I said.

Tommy arranged to stay with a friend until after graduation. He said that he knew his mom would get back in touch, so he wasn't worried about her. Now he just wanted to forget what happened. He was quiet for most of the drive to his friend's house in Regency, but I sensed he wanted to say something.

"I'm a pretty good listener," I said.

"How do you do it?" he asked.

"Do what?"

"You're mixed, right?"

"Yeah."

"Isn't it confusing not being one or the other?"

"Tommy, I can't pass, like you can. Most people think I'm something, they just don't know what. But you? You just look white. It's up to you to decide how to handle it. No one can do that for you."

"What should I do about Mr. Hunter?"

"Give it some time. He's a patient man. He spent the last 18 years looking for you and your mother. He doesn't have any expectations."

I dropped Tommy at his friend's house and gave him my card.

"If you need anything, let me know."

His smile was forced, just like Maxwell Hunter's. They looked a lot alike. His friend came out to help with Tommy's bags.

*****

Godfrey was happy to see me when I got home. I'd run out of dog food the night before and didn't have any leftovers to give him in the morning before I left. I grabbed the newspaper from the front stoop. A small envelope lay beneath it. I picked it up. There wasn't anything special about it. It looked like an invitation. Inside was a white 3"x 5" card. There was just one thing written on it.

North Downing

Since I had no idea what it meant, I went inside. Godfrey raced from the front door to the kitchen, looking back to make sure I followed. When I didn't, he came searching for me. I was in my office. Something wasn't right. My Freaky Incident file was open on my desk. There was a news clipping of my sister's murder. I looked through it. Whoever left it had circled things on a picture of the alley where her body was found. When I looked at it more closely, I realized the person hadn't actually circled anything. There wasn't anything on the ground in those places. I closed the file. Whoever got into my house knew what he was doing. Godfrey was inside all day. He would've attacked. I followed Godfrey to the kitchen. There was a bone in his dish, and a bag of dog food on the table. Damn dog took a bribe. Now, whoever it was, had my attention. I retrieved a gun I kept in a bread box on top of the refrigerator, and searched the house. No windows were broken. No locks were damaged. I returned the gun to its hiding place and poured myself a glass of scotch. Whoever got in wasn't getting in, again. I called Haithem. Within the hour, he had a team at my house and a security system installed.

Satisfied that my personal safety was no longer an issue, I settled on the couch with a bowl of popcorn, and a glass of Merlot. I popped the second season of GOT into my Blu-ray and curled up under a blanket. It'd been a long day. It was time to relax.

ABOUT THE AUTHOR

Kori Miller's creative non-fiction and short stories have been published in Fine Lines Literary Journal. She launched Back Porch Writer: The show for writers, about writers, and writing in March 2013. She's authored four books: My life in black and white: A book of experiences; Deadly Sins 1; Deadly Sins 2, and, her first children's book, titled, Dante.

Get your free copy of Kori Miller's Favorite Wordpress Plugins! Sign up for The Scoop newsletter and never miss a new release or giveaway, at www.koridmiller.com. Follow Kori on Facebook/AuthorKoriDMiller, Twitter@Kmillerwrites, Google+, LinkedIn, and Blog Talk Radio/Back Porch Writer.

Thank you for reading Deadly Sins Complete: A Dezeray Jackson Mini-Series. If you enjoyed this series, please consider leaving a review on Amazon, Goodreads, Barnes and Noble, Kobo, iTunes, and Smashwords.

HUSH

My nostrils were overwhelmed by the smell. It's that, "Oh my gawd, I know exactly what that is, but don't want to confirm it," smell. My down comforter was wrapped around my body. I was toasty warm and didn't want to move. It was dark, and I fumbled for the flashlight I kept on the table near my bed. I don't own a lamp. I did once. I lay their contemplating my options. The stench wasn't getting any better. I kicked off my blanket and got out of bed. My robe was in a pile on the floor. I picked it up and covered my now shivering body. Godfrey, my Rottie, barely stirred when I stepped over him to go to the main floor.

Here's the challenge with living in an old house -- when things fail, they completely fail. I turned off the flashlight, set it on the kitchen counter, and opened the basement door. A mixture of rotten eggs and what I can only describe as dung, wafted up the stairwell. I turned on the light. A layer of dark water covered the basement floor. There was no point in going any further. I shut the door and secured it with the eye hook. Like that was going to stop the rising tide of sewage and funk.

The kitchen lit up as the sun began its journey through the morning sky. I looked at the wall clock. It was six o'clock a.m., and too early for this kind of shit. Pun intended. I grabbed my phone book from a kitchen drawer. Yeah, I still have a phone book. I'm not ready to give up every piece of paper in favor of googling for information. Who do you call when you have a pond in your basement? If found a plumber who promised to be over before noon. I went back upstairs.

By eight-thirty a.m. I was showered and dressed in my usual jeans, black leather motorcycle boots, and a V-neck, long-sleeved T-shirt. My long, slightly kinky curls were almost dry. I grabbed a hair scrunchy and gathered my curls into a pony-tail. The phone in my office rang. I ran downstairs to answer it.

"Dezeray Jackson Investigations, how may I help you?"

The caller was named Tamara Steele. She was a criminal justice student at the University of Nebraska-Omaha. I'd met her earlier in the week while presenting a lecture at Criss library on the North campus. She requested a meeting. I'd wrapped up a few cases and didn't have anything pressing to deal with, so I agreed to meet her at Zio's Pizzeria on Dodge Street at two-thirty.

The plumber arrived as promised. He resolved the problem, billed me five hundred bucks, and left. I was feeling like I was in the wrong occupation.

I had plenty of time before the meeting, so I grabbed my workout gear, and headed to the gym for a swim. It took twenty minutes to get from my place to the "Y" on Maple Street. Omaha traffic isn't all that tough to navigate.

One of the many great things about being a private investigator are the hours. When everyone else is in an office,

I can have the pool almost to myself on a weekday. Especially, when business is slow. I know it'll pick up. Since venturing out on my own a year ago, I've had a few good cases. By good, I mean they paid enough for me to eat, and pay some bills, which is all I really need right now. When things get a little too tight, I hit up my former employer, Tracer International, for work. My good friend, Haithem Nazari, usually has a case or two waiting for an investigator.

The truth is, I'm never hurting for money. I'm a tightwad who hates dipping into my emergency fund. Over the years, I've made a few smart investments. And, when I was working for Tracer in Miami, I was able to pocket most of my check. They paid for my housing.

"Hey, Dez!" Sam greeted me from behind the check-in counter.

"Hey, Sam, how's the pool lookin' this morning?" I handed him my ID card.

"Not a soul in there, except the lifeguards, of course." Sam was short at about 5'6" and built like a bull. His ebony skin was flawless. I'd seen young ladies drool over his dimples, perfect smile, and locks. White, black, purple -- it didn't matter -- he wasn't lonely. He buzzed me into the gym.

"Have a good workout." He smiled.

I'm a sucker for dimples, too.

I went into the fitness room to stretch before my swim. That proved to be a bad idea.

"Dez!" Scott James jogged over to greet me with a kiss on the cheek.

"Scott, I didn't realize you were working today. I thought it was your day off," I said, as I kept moving toward the mat area. He followed.

"A client really needed to switch days, so here I am. It's great to see you. It seems like our schedules just aren't connecting this past month." He plopped down next to me on the mats. "You swimming today?"

"Uh huh." I started stretching.

"When you're finished, maybe we could get some lunch."

He was like a lost little puppy. "Oh, I'd like that, but I'm meeting a UNO student. She asked for some help for a class. I couldn't say 'no'." I stood up, ready to escape.

"Oh, okay. How about dinner?"

Normally, I would appreciate someone with such tenacity and willingness to buy me food. This time was different. Scott knew we were taking a break.

"Scott, look, I'm still not ready to move forward. We agreed we'd give things a little time."

"I know, it's just -- I miss you, Dez."

It was strange, looking at a man the size of Scott, appear so deflated. "Let me think about it."

I made my way to the women's locker room. He couldn't follow me in there.

*****

"Ms. Jackson!" Tamara waved at me as I entered Zio's Pizzeria. I settled into the booth across from her. The aroma of fresh-baked pizza was intoxicating. My stomach rumbled.

"Call me Dez."

"Thanks, again, for meeting me."

A young waitress set two waters onto the table, took our order, and hurried away to help another guest.

"No problem. I'm happy to help any way I can. Tell me about the case."

"Like I mentioned on the phone, it's a 2005 cold case. When I was 10, some friends and I found the body of a 13-year-old girl named Jessica Howard."

"Was this in Omaha?"

"No. I grew up in Fremont, near Valley View Golf Course. That's near where the body, sorry, where Jessica was found."

"Who was with you?"

"Kane Bryant, he's an assistant drama teacher at Fremont High School, and Sylvia and Jose Ribera. I think Sylvia is a preschool teacher in Fremont, but I'm not sure what her brother is doing. And Micah Jones. He's a student at UNO. I see him every once in a while, but we're not close." She pulled a notebook from out of her backpack.

"So, what else can you tell me?"

She flipped open the notebook. "Let me see. Okay, here it is. The detectives interviewed all of us, plus a man named Jeff Teel, her stepfather, Leo Taylor, and her mother, Cari Howard-Taylor." She looked up at me.

"What did the detectives find out about each of those people?"

"Teel was a registered sex offender, so they really went after him. I remember that. According to the reports, Jessica was sexually assaulted, but it was after she died." She paused for a moment, then added, "Teel was a necrophiliac, but the police couldn't arrest him for assaulting Jessica after she died. They didn't have enough evidence." She took a long sip from her soda.

"Where is Teel now?"

Tamara shrugged. "I have no idea. After all the publicity, he disappeared."

No surprise there. He probably took a lot of heat, and being in a small town would have made it even more difficult for him. There aren't too many people willing to hire or work with a registered sex offender.

"What about the stepfather?" I asked.

"As far as I know, he and Jessica's mother are still together. He was kind of a scary guy."

Our food arrived. She took a bite of her slice. I waited, knowing it was too hot for my taste buds. She didn't seem bothered.

"Why do you say that?"

"Jessica's family moved to the neighborhood about six months before she was killed. We knew her, but not really well. Part of the reason was because of her stepfather. We all went to her house a few times, but he -- he had a really bad temper."

I noticed that her hands trembled as she reached for her water. He must have been a special kind of asshole to have that effect so many years later.

"Tell me about Jessica."

"She disappeared June 4, 2005. We found her two weeks later on June 18. She was at the bottom of a hill in a wooded area. We were all just out and about messing around when we found her. Micah tripped over her leg. That part of the neighborhood is hilly. There're lots of trees and bushes. We hung out there a lot. I don't know why we didn't see her sooner. I guess things really do happen for a reason." She fiddled with her straw as she explained.

"Were you the youngest?"

"No, Jose and I were both 10. Kane was 13, Sylvia was 12, and Micah was 11. We were all pretty messed up for a while after that, except Kane. He was the oldest, so he handled it better than we did, I think. For a while, we talked about it a lot. All the time, it seemed like." She took another drink. "Then, I don't know, it was like everyone just wanted to move on, ya know? But, it always bothered me."

"Have you tried talking to Jessica's parents?"

"I've called a few times, but Mrs. Taylor keeps saying she's told the police everything and can't remember anything else."

"What about Mr. Taylor?"

"He was never home when I called."

"What about your friends?"

"We aren't really friends anymore. I've left messages, but no one's called me back. I think they just want to forget about it."

"Don't you?"

She thought about that for a minute.

"I can't."

"I'm confused about something," I said.

Tamara looked at me, her eyes widened.

"Most CJ interns don't get cases to work. They're usually on the bench taking direction. In my experience, there's a lot more oversight. How'd you get assigned a cold case?"

She shifted in her seat and her right hand raised to cover that little space between the collar bones. Then, she bit her lip.

"It just isn't right," she said.

"What? Crimes go unsolved all the time. Nebraska has pretty good size list. So, how did you get involved in this?"

"I feel like I owe it to Jessica. No one should die the way she did."

"Tamara, you're not answering my question. Were you assigned this cold case?"

She looked down at her empty plate, and said, "No."

"What do you want me to do?"

"I just want to see if we can find any new information. The lead investigator is busy, and Jessica's case isn't getting any attention. It hasn't for a long time."

I finished my slices, and was already feeling that warm, happy feeling in my belly.

"You're not supposed to touch the cases, Tamara. A shit-storm could rain down on you if you pursue this. Any hopes of a CJ career you have could disappear."

"I know."

"And, you're willing to just throw it away? What kind of law are you planning to study?"

"Criminal."

"Really? You might need to re-think that if you go this route."

"I know, but I can't work in that office, knowing that Jessica's case isn't being investigated."

I mulled this over. Nothing kept me from helping, except the pro bono nature of it. Pro bono doesn't add to my bank account, but I needed more karma points.

"All right, I'll give you a week of my time to see if we can come up with anything."

"That's great! Thanks, Dez."

"You're welcome, but I haven't done anything, yet. And, don't keep snooping in the Howard case file."

*****

"Hey, Dez!" I looked back as I got out of my Jeep. Patrick Murphy got off of his Harley and strolled up the driveway.

"Where the hell did you come from?"

"Around."

"You just getting' back?" Murphy was an ex-Marine gone gun-for-hire kinda guy, but without the gun. He was more into hand-to-hand combat. Private security was a good fit for him.

"Yeah."

He followed me to the front door. I could hear Godfrey on the other side, pacing.

"Hang on a sec. I need to deal with Godfrey."

"What? He loves me."

"You don't remember the last time you came over unexpected?"

"He was just playing."

"Stay here."

The last time Murphy showed up, he walked in without knocking. Godfrey barreled through the kitchen to the front door, and tackled him. By the time I realized what had happened, Godfrey's jaw was closed around Murphy's neck. My dog tolerated guests; He didn't actually like them unless they came bearing gifts.

I went inside, placed Godfrey's food dishes on the back deck, and sent him outside.

"All clear."

Murphy came in and found his way to the kitchen.

"You got any beer?"

"In the fridge."

"Scotch?"

"By the stove. What's up with you?" I was leaning against the counter watching him get his beer and Scotch.

"What do you mean?" He found a glass and poured his drink.

I stared at him. Clearly, he was a bit slow on the uptake this evening.

"Where the hell have you been all this time?"

"I had a job."

"And it required that you leave in the middle of the night?"

"About that, I've been meaning to talk to you."

"Shut it. It's been almost a year, Murphy."

I pushed past him to get myself a glass. I filled it, and left the kitchen.

After a few beats, Murphy joined me in the living room. He knew me well enough to know that following right away might get him into more trouble. I sat in my favorite over-size chair with my feet propped up on the ottoman. He sat on the couch.

I waited.

"Something came up, and yeah, it was in the middle of the night."

"And you couldn't pick up a phone or shoot me a message in the past eight or so months?"

"No, I couldn't." His eyes met mine.

I sipped my scotch. Murphy was a straight shooter. That was one thing that never changed about him.

"Where were you?"

"Can't say."

"Not stateside, then."

"Not stateside."

"Is it over?"

"Yeah, it's over."

"You have some serious making up to do."

"I know."

I ordered Chinese takeout. We stayed up late catching up. Around two in the morning, I kicked his sorry ass out. Making up with me ain't that easy.

A Conversation with

Kori D. Miller

Q. Why do you write about the deadly sins?

A. In the beginning, I was simply trying to come up with an easy way to create story ideas. It occurred to me, after watching the news one morning, that every crime is linked to one or more of the deadly sins. I'd found my hook.

Q. Where did you get the ideas for the stories in Deadly Sins I and II?

A. Some of them came to me after watching news stories. Others are from experiences with people I've met over the years. And, some are the result of me playing the "what if" game. I ask myself, "what if x happened, then what?" and continue until I flesh out a story idea.

Q. Dezeray Jackson is a strong lead character. When will we see her fatal flaw?

A. Throughout the series, more and more of Dez's personality gets revealed, and not just her physical strength or impatience. My intention is to create a female character with whom readers can relate on a few levels -- a woman they'd like to emulate. Dez owns her life. She never apologizes for who she is.

Q. What do you have in common with Dezeray Jackson?

A. We're both tenacious, have a low tolerance for BS, play pool, and are martial artists. That's where the similarities end. Ideologically, we're pretty far apart.

Q. Why is Omaha, NE the backdrop for your stories?

A. The simple answer is, I grew up there. Writing about places in Omaha still requires some research, but it's basically familiar territory. And, I do like Omaha. Growing up there, I couldn't wait to move away, but I think that's normal. Having traveled and lived all over the US, I made a conscious choice to return to Nebraska. Like other cities, it has its negatives and positives. I want to share my view on those things through my books.

Q. Dezeray Jackson is a private investigator. Have you ever done that job?

A. No, but I did study criminal justice in college long enough to realize it wasn't a good fit for me. I spent ten years working in some aspect of human/social services. This experience gave me a unique view into worlds I otherwise wouldn't have encountered. I know several people working in law enforcement, and often ask them procedural questions. In the case of "The Hood," mentioned in *Buyer Beware*, I needed to know a specific location in Lincoln where drug deals happen. I know a Lincoln police officer and he was able to shed some light on that for me. Writing fiction often requires some research.